Leaves

on the Line

An anthology of *fiction* from
the MA in Creative Writing at the
University of East Anglia

Centre for Creative and Performing Arts

Published by the Centre for Creative and Performing Arts,
The University of East Anglia, Norwich.
Printed in Great Britain by Page Bros, Norwich
Set in Linotype Caslon Old Face 2.

British Library Cataloguing in Publication Data
A Catalogue Record for this book is available from the British Library
Leaves on the Line
I.—
II. Centre for Creative and Performing Arts
—

ISBN 0-95/5009-3-7

acknowledgements

The editors would like to thank Mike Oakes, Andy Vargo, Jane Chittenden, Phoebe Phillips, Anastacia Tohill, Jon Cook, the Eastern Arts Board, and the Norfolk Institute of Art and Design, for their help and advice.

Leaves *on the* Line

Leaves on the Line is an anthology of short stories and extracts from longer works by students of the MA in Creative Writing course at the University of East Anglia in 1991-92.

Leaves on the Line was edited and produced by Neil Church, Archie Clifford, Beatrice Kirsch, Tasha Pym and David Rhymes

contents

Rose Tremain

Introduction

L *eaves on the Line* is the fourth anthology of stories to come from the students on the MA Course in Creative Writing at the University of East Anglia.

The first collection, *Unthank*, was published in 1989 and it originated not with either Malcolm Bradbury or myself, but with four of the 1988/89 students. Since then, the Course has presented *Exposure* (1990) and *The Word Party* (1991). Each year, the book is funded by UEA's Centre for Creative and Performing Arts under the guidance of Jon Cook and produced by those students taking the publishing course at the Norwich Institute of Art and Design – this year, Neil Church, Archie Clifford, Beatrice Kirsch, Tasha Pym and David Rhymes.

For most of the writers represented here, this is their first appearance in print. They offer the title to the reader courtesy of British Rail who, last year, were unable to cope with autumn, but it relates also to another season - to that difficult early spring in a writer's life when private composition becomes public critical property, to that moment when the creative self is 'laid on the line'.

Much can be said about the aims and achievements of the MA Course by looking closely at the anthology titles. The mysterious word 'unthank' is known intimately by the 100,000 inhabitants of the city of Norwich and to almost no one outside it. The Unthank Road leads west out of the town centre towards the University. This inaugural title serves, then, to remind the reader of two important facts: firstly, that the MA Course in Creative Writing here at UEA, founded by the late Sir Angus Wilson and by Malcolm Bradbury in 1970, was the first of its kind in this country; that out of a sleepy East Anglian city came a radical idea about the nature of the writer's craft. Secondly, *Unthank* reminds us that, in the late 20th Century, young writers are working in a publishing climate so shaped by the cult of the bestseller that their commitment to serious fiction is likely to remain 'unthanked' unless or until it starts to capture a large readership. One of the most important benefits the Course offers the new writer, therefore, is a kind of temporary shelter from the market-place, a protected environment in which a new voice can be heard and encouraged, sometimes even before it has truly heard itself.

How is it heard and encouraged? The second anthology title, *Exposure*, gives some clue to this. 'Exposure' refers not only to first time publication, but also to weekly group scrutiny, to the exposure to criticism sustained by the writers in the lively Tuesday workshops. In these sometimes passionate and fiery discussions, the writer is face to face with the unsentimental reader, the constructive critic who is willing to admire the fine quality of an emperor's garments, but who also dares to identify nakedness.

The third anthology, *The Word Party*, suggests, I think, the joy and relief felt by the course participants at the ending of the isolation in which they have previously been working. Writing is always - must always be - a solitary endeavour, but no moment in a writer's life is as lonely as his/her first years, when there is no readership waiting beyond the study door and no certainty that there ever will be one. Young writers are haunted by the suspicion that they are launched upon a mad enterprise. Bring them into a group, however, (a group of the similarly haunted) and much of their unease and self-doubt will disappear. And at UEA, they have access, too, to the sociable side of the writing life: to passionate pub chat, to crowded public readings by well known writers, to parties for agents and publishers. By the end of each year, most course participants agree that this aspect of the MA has sustained them and helped to keep away their private demons.

In 1992, the group is larger than usual: sixteen members, as opposed to ten or twelve. This was dictated by the high standard of submissions, making us reluctant to turn talented people away, simply on the grounds of numbers. Much of this talent is on show here, in *Leaves on the Line*. It is discernible via widely differing approaches to subject and to language. The gap (linguistic, ontological, aesthetic) that separates, say, August Braxton's engagingly flamboyant *Sermons in Stone* from Karin Hurst's beautifully understated *This Place* is very wide. Joanne Gooding's ghostly *Interior Designs* is worlds away in conception and preoccupation from Matthew Whyman's fable of deception, *Spreading the Word*. Jane Harris from Scotland and Adam Campbell from Jamaica both reveal in their stories an acute understanding of and a profound debt to the cultures that have nurtured them, but these places and these fictions are, quite literally, worlds apart. While many of the writers in *Leaves* - Neil Church, Archie Clifford, David Rhymes, Patricia Debney, Tasha Pym and the prize winning Sarah Gracie - are working imaginatively in the realist tradition, others - Kirkham Jackson, Katherine Finkelstein, Simon Christmas, C.M. Rafferty - are engaged in lively experimentation.

The short story, here, is moving forwards in many different moods and modes, thus effectively dismantling the notion that the UEA MA Course produces a homogeneous 'stable' of writers who are 'taught' to write in a certain way. They are not taught to write in a certain way. They are not taught to write at all. This is to patronise them and to misunderstand the raison d'être of the Course. These sixteen are people already committed to being writers. What they have competed for (the ratio of applicants to the course to available places is about ten to one) is the sanctuary of a year's protected time, in which they can begin to hear what it is they want to say and find the means with which to say it.

Good writing is a synthesis between inspiration and craft. These stories are the work of a talented group coming to terms with this simple truth.

Sarah Gracie

The Grasshouse

When Uncle Jack arrived at his friends' house for lunch, Samantha was not immediately there.

'Oh, don't worry,' said Annette. 'She's been waiting for you all morning: Uncle Jack this, Uncle Jack that. She'll appear in a minute.'

'Yes,' said Bill. 'You're a great favourite. I could get jealous, you know, if it went any further.'

Jack had been a favourite with Samantha for some years now. He had watched her grow from a squalling puck-eyed baby to a crook-toothed, blue-eyed bombshell of six, who enchanted him with her wit and vitality. He enjoyed her company now perhaps more than that of her parents, his old friends, whose conversation had become too full of mortgages, promotions, and cars. He would joke that none of his girlfriends were a patch on her, and that he remained single in honour of her.

'So what's she up to these days?' he asked, putting her present, a very fetching bikini made out of pink lurex, on the table.

'Oh, grasshouses,' said Bill with a smile. 'That's all the rage now.'

'Grasshouses?'

'You take the cuttings from the lawn, arrange them in lines, and make houses out of them. She spends hours at it.'

'Literally,' said Annette, rolling out a ball of pastry to the edge of her board, then when a rip appeared, rolling it up again, kneading it carefully, and rolling it out again. 'Hours.'

'Well,' said Bill. 'She's off to school soon. I suppose that'll change things a bit.'

'And a good thing too,' Annette said, rolling the pastry finely again to the edge of the board, her mouth pulled down at the side in a small dry tuck. 'Get a bit of reality into her head.'

Bill sighed and looked mock-melancholy. 'Annette thinks we're spoiling her. Too many presents. Too many games. She thinks Sammy's a bit short on the old reality principle.'

Jack shivered. 'Ugh!' he said, and thought wistfully that if Annette rolled much more pastry she'd lose her looks completely. 'As little as possible of that. As little for as long as possible.'

Shortly afterwards Samantha herself appeared in the doorway, dressed in a pair of knickers and a large white hat. She had a small ripe body, gold as a stalk of wheat, which hovered at a mid-way point between the distended drum-like curves of the toddler and the willowy verticals of a young girl. Her hair hung down in blond ropes from beneath the brim of the hat.

'Samantha!' her mother said, and put down the rolling pin with some impatience. 'How did you get that hat? I put it as far up as – you must have gone right up to the top of my cupboard!'

And Annette moved across the room, took off the hat, and began dusting it free of the wisps of dried grass which had stuck to it.

Samantha looked disappointed. A set expression came into her face, and she stared down, curling her bare foot into the ground.

'She was dressing up for Jack,' Bill said now with a smile. 'Weren't you Sammy?'

Everyone laughed.

But Samantha remained silent, her eyes cast down and her expression hovering on the brink of serious offense.

'Here,' said Jack now, leaning forward. 'I brought you a present.'

Samantha took the present cautiously. Peeling off the fine layer of tissue, she uncovered the bikini. Then she looked at it with a rapt concentration of pleasure, fascination, horror – Jack could not tell which.

'Oh, a bikini!' said Annette, who always wore elegant and respectable one-pieces. 'How daring! What a grown-up girl!'

And Bill added: 'Yes, you mustn't go on the beach in that Sammy, or you'll have all the men in a terrible state.'

There was another round of laughter, prolonged, at the image of Samantha strutting down the beach in her bikini, all gazes upon her.

But two tears now appeared imminent at the edges of her eyes.

Jack was suddenly ashamed. He leaned forward. 'But I hear you're making grasshouses these days?' he said, in his gentlest voice.

A small nod.

'I'd love to see them.'

She didn't immediately reply.

'Oh come on Sammy,' Bill said affably. 'Stop playing hard to get.' And then to Jack: 'She's been wanting to show you her grasshouses all morning. Nobody else has been allowed near the lawn, in case they tread on them. Go on Samantha, why don't you take Uncle Jack down the garden and show him. He's dying to see them, aren't you Jack?'

Outside, it was a brilliant day. The sun shone fiercely on the vines which looped the house, the whitewashed walls, and the red bricks of the terrace, turning everything into a jumbled heat-refracted maze of colour. Beside him, Samantha was subdued, and trod along with her eyes cast down in front of her.

Jack looked for something to say.

'It was a very nice hat,' he said, after a pause. 'It suited you. You have a bright future in hats.'

And then after another pause. 'It was silly about the bikini. You don't have to wear it. We'll get you a proper one-piece some time, eh? You and me. A very smart one. Very elegant. Very *respectable*.'

It seemed to do the trick, for a short while later a hot little hand arrived in his own, nestling there calmly, and breathing in and out, like some creature with tiny diaphanous lungs. Jack was overwhelmed by a sensation of protectiveness, almost painful.

They plodded in silence through the hot grass.

'Watch out!' she said suddenly. 'You're treading on a wall.'

Sure enough, when he looked down, Jack saw that he had been about to tread on a small mound of dried grass, about three inches high and four wide. As his eye followed this mound, he saw that it stretched out in linear fashion for several yards to the end of the lawn, then took a sharp right and continued at right angles for another few yards until it came to the wall. In fact, as his eye blinking into the sun soon gathered, the whole lawn was criss-crossed with a wavering grid of some complexity, inside which there were more grids, and then more.

'Oh, *very* impressive,' he said. '*Very* elaborate.' And Samantha, beside him, looked pleased as Punch.

She guided him round the edge of the largest rectangle, until they reached a small break in the cuttings, about a foot wide.

'This is the front door,' she said. 'And these are the steps. You must wipe your feet.'

Jack did as instructed, wiping his feet elaborately on the lawn, and they entered a narrow passage between two rows of grass. The passage was about a foot wide, wide enough for her to skip along in her bare feet, but too narrow for him to negotiate without continually threatening the mounds of grass.

'I think I'll take my shoes off, on your nice carpet and everything,' he said.

She giggled. He bent down now and took his shoes off, leaving them carefully side by side at the door. Then he trod, in his socks, down the passage, feeling the hot grass prickle between his toes.

Samantha now became proprietorial and imperious, a version of her mother in miniature. She went ahead, gesturing at things expansively and proudly.

'And this is the hall,' she said. 'And this is the kitchen. And here's the dining room and here's the sitting room. And this is the sink and this is the study and these are the stairs. Come *on*!' she said, turning back and frowning at him impatiently. For he had fallen behind, still trying to find a way of walking without destroying the walls.

'It's time to go upstairs.'

Jack caught up and they plodded laboriously round a winding curve of grass which represented stairs, he puffing obligingly to simulate the gradient, and then came out at another grid, which was at some distance from the first.

'This is upstairs,' she said. 'And these are the bedrooms.'

And then she was off again. 'This is my bedroom and this is the spare bedroom and this is the bathroom and this is the airing cupboard and this is the other bathroom and this is the big bedroom.'

They arrived in a large rectangle which contained a rectangle almost as big as itself.

'And what's this?' Jack said, pointing at it.

'That's the big bed.' Samantha had her back turned, and was about to start off again. But Jack paused, not wanting to move on so quickly.

It seemed a very beautiful bed, situated close to the flowers

7

which grew by the wall, and on a slight uptilt of the grass, so that the heavy crimson blooms of the peony heads dripped over onto it. The grass was particularly thick there, untouched by the mower, and threaded with clumps of daisies and violets. Across the whole area hung a sweet hot smell of lavender from the herb beds, which mingled headily with the tang of cut grass.

'Oh!' he yawned. 'How tired I am!' And abruptly he lay down.

Samantha giggled and looked at him. 'Your feet are too long!'

'Well, that's no good. A man has to have somewhere to put his feet,' he said. 'Change it!'

She paused as if considering whether this was admissable, then bent swiftly and rearranged the grass in a neat line to take account of his feet.

Then she stood looking down, clearly enjoying her sudden superiority of height.

'You look silly,' she giggled.

'Oh no, not silly,' said Jack. 'Not silly.' He paused. 'But I am lonely in my big bed. And the nights are so dark. I need someone to keep me company.'

Another giggle, and she had lain down beside him.

Now he pretended to snore loudly. And as he did so, he looked through narrowed eyes into hers. It was a strange vision. He could see the whole of her fine flower-like face in acute focus, pressed up close to his. He saw the freckles scattered over her nose, the super-fine skin with its sheen of translucence, her chip tooth. He felt the warmth of her breath, as it reached him in milky outpuffs; and her eyes, between their fringe of lashes, seemed to stab at him, like a shaft of blue glass, or the flash of a kingfisher's wing.

He felt an overwhelming desire to do something, hold her close, kiss her.

So, abruptly, he leaned over and pressed his lips to her stomach, blowing a loud snorting kiss that tickled her and made her giggle furiously.

'No!' she squealed. 'No, no! You don't do that! You don't do that!'

He continued, making her wriggle and squeal, until she panted for breath.

'No! No! You don't do that!' she repeated. 'When you're in the big bed.'

He paused, motion arrested. 'What?'

She repeated, panting. 'You don't do that – when you're in the big bed.'

He reclined slowly onto his elbow with a sense that he shouldn't inquire further, that to do so would be to take advantage somehow in a wholly unacceptable way. But after several moments hesitation, he couldn't stop himself.

'And what *do* you do?' he said softly. 'When you're in the big bed.'

The suddenness of the change alarmed him. The giggling was gone in a breath, like an instantaneous suffocation. The wriggling and panting had vanished. And she lay before him, like a small stiff doll, with her face pulled up into an expression of rigid piety and frigidity, for all the world like a tiny replica of Annette at her most tense and unhappy.

'That's what you do,' she said, through tight lips. 'When you're in the big bed.'

Jack was suddenly sad, awash with a tidal sensation of his own age and folly.

Contemplating her for a moment, he leaned over and planted a chaste kiss on her forehead. 'C'mon,' he said. 'It's time we went back.'

She hopped up, and dusting the grass off her knee, looked bewildered, as if she had been punished for something, she knew not what.

And then in silence together, her hand held quietly in his, they made their way back through the heat of the day towards the shuttered house.

Adam Belgrave Campbell

An Unrestricted View

In the darkness of his hut, Good-Luck Chitembe realised suddenly that he was awake again. The thoughts which rushed around his head, like seeds in a gourd rattle, had been pursuing him relentlessly all night, in and out of sleep, blurring, for a moment anyway, the distinction between one and the next.

He raised himself up on his elbows and squinted through fatigue-thickened lids into the chill blackness of the Zambian night, to see if he could detect the diffuse grey of the coming dawn. Seeing nothing of it, he closed his eyes, fell back onto his narrow bed and was straight back into that semi-conscious world of half-sleep.

The reason for his interrupted sleep – for before now, Good-Luck had been known to snore his way through an entire evening of end-of-crop celebrations – lay about three-quarters of a mile away behind the small but imposing hill. This *kopje*, which sat squat and impenetrable between the farmhouse and the township, tended to obscure, at night as in the day, the one from the other. However, tonight its effect, on Good-Luck at least, was nil. For Elisabeth Dunlop, her hair the colour of sun-bleached straw and her eyes a swimming pool blue, had dominated his thoughts since the previous evening, since before he had left the farmhouse in fact, where he worked as cook, head-cleaner, sometime-nanny and butler and, on days like yesterday, all of them rolled into one.

Yesterday had been a big day for her. Her husband, Ralston, a cane farmer – one of the country's biggest – had invited the General Manager of the Sugar Company and his wife round for dinner: a kind of social precursor to the new year's working relationship.

'Now, Good-Luck,' she had said at the first opportunity that morning, 'this is an important man. Prices, quotas, you name it, he's got a hand in it. Well, I don't need to remind you, you've been through it before. How many times?'

He cast his mind back. 'About four madam.'

'Four.' She rolled the number idly around her tongue for a while. Then she was back, hurtling through her list of jobs to be done, pausing only occasionally to make sure he was still with her; and if he wasn't, then he pretended to be anyway.

The conveyor was rolling.

All morning she was edgy, beads of sweat forming on her upper lip as she shooed the cleaners mercilessly around the house. Her mood swung between exasperation and elation with the consistency of a pendulum, the shifts provoked by the slightest thing.

At eleven thirty, the electricity went off for the second time and she told Good-Luck that she was dismissing Patricia, the woman who did the vacuuming, for not having foreseen this and done it the day before. While he was trying to persuade her that Patricia had no control over the electricity company, Henry, their ever-present Rottweiler, left an unusually dislocated turd beneath the dining table.

'Grace!' she shrieked when it was pointed out to her. 'What have you been feeding him? This is your fault! Now get in there and clean it up.'

Grace burst into tears.

Moments later, the electricity came back on and suddenly Elisabeth Dunlop was reinstating Patricia with such vigour that Good-Luck thought she might hug her.

He took much of this in with an habitual nonchalance. From where he stood, he could see how she, in her early thirties and a good twenty-five years younger than her husband, might feel under pressure from some of the situations which his job threw up and why, therefore, she sometimes reacted the way she did.

However, as the day wore on, her demands became more and more exotic and he began to sense that there was something different about this particular dinner.

'Good-Luck – those flower-stalks are too long; please get some new ones cut.

'Good-Luck – there are too many fork marks in the pastry. Oh, and get Grace to make the beds again. Well, you never know, they may want to look around.

'Good-Luck – get Patricia to run the toothbrush between those tiles.'

Now *that*, he thought, was something she hadn't done since her mother, who thought she lived in a mud hut, had come up from South Africa for a visit.

It got so bad that, by mid-afternoon, all of the other staff had been to see him, to see if he could do something about it. He promised to try. So he pulled her to one side, appalled by his daring. 'Madam,' he suggested, 'why don't you have a small sleep this afternoon, to be fresh for this evening.'

She eyed him suspiciously for a moment and he began to worry that he'd misread the situation and overstepped the mark. Then suddenly she agreed, 'You're right Good-Luck, I am feeling a little tired. Thanks. You'll make sure my instructions are carried out to the letter.'

'Of course madam,' he exhaled slowly.

Finally, everything was ready: not a napkin, not a pillow-slip out of place. And still Good-Luck didn't know what was so special about this dinner, what set it apart, in Elisabeth Dunlop's mind at least, from all the others.

And still she didn't say.

The Dunlops were dressing when Good-Luck heard the car

approach the gate and come to a stop. He went to the front door and stood watching as a black Mercedes rolled up the floodlit driveway, unfurling cumuliform dust-clouds self-importantly behind. It swept through a wide arc to a majestic halt before the front step.

The driver climbed out and opened the rear door. When he saw the passengers, Good-Luck stiffened in disbelief beneath his starch-crisp uniform. His palms became sticky and his collar suddenly felt tight around his neck. His thoughts were highly charged: Never would he have imagined this! His wildest guesses hadn't even come close. The Dunlops never entertained Africans! *Never!* And yet, the two people standing on the front step, he in a safari suit and she in a floral print dress, were undoubtedly African; that is to say, black, like himself.

He stayed like that, inert in the doorway as though screwed to the floor, until, to his added surprise, he felt the Dunlops push impatiently past him and rush down the steps to greet them like old friends. Then they were steering the couple in, hands on their elbows, as if they expected them to turn and run at the first opportunity. The sight of the four of them almost on top of him spurred him into action, but on the point of a well-worn 'Good evening sir, madam,' he found that he couldn't get the words out and instead retreated hastily into the kitchen.

There, he busied himself with the preparations as if to deaden, by strenuous activity, some of the shock he was feeling. He checked the roast in the oven, set a couple of saucepans of water to boil and began to make a Bearnaise sauce. But he fumbled the eggs, dropping one, and then split two of the yolks while trying to separate them. Slicing the shallots with none of his usual skill but all of his usual speed, he almost sliced off the tips of his fingers. All the while his mind was on those people in the next room.

Elisabeth Dunlop came crashing through the swing door.

'Good-Luck, we've decided to start immediately,' she said, trying to take a deep breath and swallow at the same time. In response to his raised eyebrows she said, 'Don't ask me why. They're up early tomorrow, or something.'

'But the toast madam. It is not ready.'

'Oh bloody hell, man!' she cried, biting her lip in frustration. 'Do we really need – ? Oh, never mind. Just get it out there as soon as it's ready.'

She started to leave, then stopped as she caught sight of her reflection in the window. Patting at the hair piled high on her head, she said, 'What about the Bearnaise?' But before he could answer she turned and saw the yolks spilling languidly out of the shells onto the counter and the smashed egg at her feet. 'Oh, for goodness' sake, Good-Luck! Don't screw this up!' she both ordered and implored and, with one final glance in the window, she disappeared.

When the pate and toast were ready, he opened up the hatch in the wall and passed the plates through. On the other side, he recovered them and placed one in front of each person, spreading the napkins in their laps as he went. They were arranged around the table – man, woman, man, woman – with husbands and wives facing each other.

Elisabeth Dunlop was talking to the General Manager about Rottweilers while her husband tried to engage the other woman.

'So, how easily did you find us?' asked Ralston Dunlop, taking a large sip from his glass.

'Pardon me?' said the African woman.

'I said, how easily – ?'

'Darling!' Elisabeth Dunlop broke off to scold him, smiling, 'They do have a driver you know.'

'Of course they do. Silly question. Sorry.' He laughed nervously and reached for the glass again but pulled back sharply when he saw that it was empty.

The food served, Good-Luck cast his eye over the table to make sure everything was where it should be and, in so doing, he saw the African woman bent over, scrutinising the three knives in front of her. Her husband was busy spreading pâté, but Good-Luck could see that the Dunlops were watching her, wondering, he was sure, if she knew which one to use. He flinched when he saw them both reach forward, poised to tell her, when she suddenly picked it up and said to Elisabeth Dunlop, who was retracting her hand as though from a flame, 'Your silver is beautiful Elisabeth, where did you get it?'

'Er . . .'

'Johannesburg, we got the set in Johannesburg,' chipped in Ralston Dunlop.

Back in the kitchen snatches of their conversation drifted in to Good-Luck through the half-open hatch. The subject matter was routine enough: the rains were late, poaching in Kafue game park was on the up, as were the food shortages in Lusaka. But still he could sense the Dunlops' awkwardness. He could hear it in their laughter which was over-loud, forced. And though he could think of no reason why he should be embarrassed, he found he was. He was embarrassed for the African couple, embarrassed for the Dunlops, embarrassed for himself even.

At a signal from Elisabeth Dunlop he began to ferry the main course dishes through from the kitchen, watching as he did so her furtive eyes following her guests' every move – dainty with their napkins, polite with their helpings. She was, it seemed, willing their delicacy, their casual observation of dinner table protocol. As, he was both alarmed and ashamed to discover, was he.

Ralston Dunlop opened a bottle of wine. He poured a dribble into the General Manager's glass, hesitated for a second and then continued to pour. Then he must have thought again because he stopped, colouring slightly, leaving the glass half-full.

'There you go,' he said, his voice full of camaraderie, 'What do you think of that?'

The man lifted the glass into the light, then reached for the bottle, handed to him by a stunned Ralston Dunlop, and studied the label. He sniffed the wine long and hard in the silence.

'My husband considers himself a bit of a connoisseur,' mocked the African woman lightly.

Finally, he tasted it, and winced.

'As I thought, Ralston,' he said gravely, 'this wine is corked.'

A dazed Ralston Dunlop hastened out of the room to get another, not even stopping to check for himself.

As the wine flowed, however, and the evening flowed along with it, things began to loosen up. Gradually, Good-Luck came to the conclusion that what he'd found unnerving at first was in fact quite thrilling: an African couple at the Dunlop dinner table! It was more than thrilling, it was astounding! A little later, he heard the General Manager's wife, through the hatch, praising the consistency of the bearnaise sauce. Her houseboy, she said, could never get it quite like that. His chest swelled with pride.

By the time he wheeled the cheese trolley through the swing door then, he was much relaxed, as much, he supposed, as he ever would be, considering the circumstances. He stacked the dessert bowls next to the hatch and began to walk the trolley from one person to the next.

It was the sudden clarity with which he heard the occasional and high-pitched squeak of the trolley wheels which made him realise that the room had fallen silent around him. And in the silence, he felt curiously vulnerable, as though he were under the scrutiny of all four of them. The memory that, until now, he had been the observer and they the observed heightened his sensitivity. He kept his eyes downwards, trying to concentrate only on cutting cheese, telling himself repeatedly that it didn't matter. But still he felt those eyes on him. And despite himself he couldn't help looking up, just to check. He swept his gaze round the table in a rapid arc and saw that he was wrong: only the African man was looking. His eyes caught the other's and held them for a couple of seconds, knowing as he did so that he had strayed one second longer than he would have dared – desired even – had those eyes belonged to a European.

An instant later, he regretted it.

'And what's your name, sir?' the man asked him.

He cursed himself for having given in to his curiosity and instead of answering, he looked stupidly across at Mr Dunlop and then Mrs Dunlop.

'Go on then,' said Ralston Dunlop, taunting gently, 'what's wrong? Cat got your tongue?'

He felt his cheeks burning. 'Good-Luck,' he replied at last, hoping this would be the end of it.

'And how do they treat you here, Good-Luck?' The man's face broke into a broad grin now.

The silence came again.

He felt as though he were caught in a spider's web, all twisted and stuck, struggling silently and without success. Then he saw, with more pity than satisfaction, that the smiles on the faces of Ralston and Elisabeth Dunlop had frozen and were beginning to fade.

'They treat me very well, sir. Yes sir, very well,' he stuttered the compliment at last, and added freely, with abandon, 'The best employers I've ever had sir,' before scuttling from the room. At the swing door he heard the man remark, 'He would say that, wouldn't he?' and then the ice was broken and the four of them began to laugh.

Compared with this, the rest of the evening passed uneventfully, but when midnight came and the guests were about to leave, Good-Luck was grateful for its end. He'd had enough surprises for one night, and it was with a certain sense of satisfaction that he heard the goodbyes, the slamming of the car door and the revving engine.

Ralston and Elisabeth Dunlop came back inside glowing, praising each other for a job well done. Good-Luck could hear the relief in their voices. The truth was, he felt it himself, for only now, in the aftermath, did he appreciate just how tense it had all been. It made him feel good, this release, and as he cleared away the last of the things he felt, for once, that he had been a part of the evening, a member in some small way of the team which turned this farm over from year to year. For after all, he told himself, this had been a successful business dinner, which he had helped to bring off.

'Good-Luck handled it all pretty well, didn't he darling?' he overheard Ralston Dunlop say in the hall. 'You'd better have a word.'

Yes, he thought again, a successful dinner.

'Hey, and what about that wine?' she said.

Ralston Dunlop laughed. 'I know, who'd have guessed? *Corked,*' he exaggerated the General Manager's accent and they both giggled.

'The funny thing is Liz, they were so . . . well, refined I suppose, that by the end, I'd almost forgotten they were *kaffirs*. Still, not for another year, thank God!'

A moment later, Elisabeth Dunlop came breezing into the kitchen, all smiles and compliments, everything now that she hadn't been during the day. 'Well done Good-Luck! That was marvellous. Just what the doctor ordered. You were fantastic, man!' She couldn't congratulate him enough. 'You were really on top form tonight, man, I mean it! And what you said about us, that was really sweet.'

'Just because I said it doesn't mean I meant it,' he said in a low voice, turning from his position at the sink to face her. His eyes were burning and he knew that the anger showed in his face.

He stared at her hard then, in a way that he would never before have dared, straight into her alcohol-moist eyes, which betrayed first a look of shock, then incomprehension and then of knowing as she realised he'd overheard. Still he held her gaze, his teeth gritted, watching with grim satisfaction as she moved from realisation to embarrassment. He knew that he had stepped well beyond the normal bounds of their relationship, but it felt right. His courage was instinctive; the situation had a certain feel about it – a taste almost, or a smell. He just knew that tonight, maybe tomorrow too, he could get away with this. And nor, it seemed, was his instinct unfounded, for neither did she break the look. Her eyes hardened too and her stare was also unwavering as she recovered some of her usual poise.

Time geared down to a crawl. Good-Luck could see, at the edge of his focus, her lips moving nervously over one another, becoming slightly moist. Her hair was rumpled and a ringlet had fallen down, curling under her chin. He thought he detected a shortening in her breathing, a flush beginning in her face. A rapid surge of emotion overtook him. He had a powerful desire to reach out and brush the curl back behind her ear. His own cheeks became hot and a sweat broke out on his brow as he began to stiffen beneath his belly. Still their eyes held; they were practically joined. But with the beginnings of a physical response, he found it harder to maintain the stare, and soon he felt her eyes also beginning to falter. His confidence began to slip, the suspension of consciousness began to break.

At that moment of instability, he was forced to drop his own gaze, and his eyes slipped down her face, past her reddened neck, the goose pimples beneath her collar bones and across the fold of her blouse. He saw that beneath the material her nipples had hardened to little points. Quickly he looked up at her face again, wondering what he might see there, but the moment had passed. Her eyes looked past him now, they had glazed over.

Suddenly she was retreating, suggesting that he finish the clearing up the next morning, it was late. Thanks again for his help, but please to go now, he must be tired. Then she vanished into the blackness of the long corridor, leaving him alone and blinking beneath the brightness of the fluorescent strip.

*

In his hut, Good-Luck raised his head up from the bed suddenly, and at once realised that, this time, he really had fallen asleep. What had been black through the open door before was now a dull grey, tinged towards the horizon with an intensifying orange. He knew at once that he was late for work but as he had no watch he wasn't sure exactly how late. He always relied on his body-clock to wake him and he usually found that by the time he had got to the farmhouse, boiled the water, walked the teapot and tray down the long corridor and knocked lightly on the heavy door, it was around six-thirty. But today, his routine had been thrown.

He got up and dressed. Emerging from the hut, he blinked in the strengthening light, then stood for a moment rubbing his eyes. Around him, the gridiron collection of fog-grey huts, like giant tin cans buried up to their middles, was silent. Only two women were up, crouched down on the hard-compacted brown earth outside one of the huts, making a fire to boil water they had collected from the standpipe at the base of the *kopje*. They acknowledged him briefly, '*Mullibwange*,' as he went by and soon his bare feet found the dirt track which led to the main gate of the farm compound.

He walked along it slowly, reflecting once again on the events of the previous evening, which had robbed him of his sleep. His initial excitement had soon turned to panic when he began to think things through properly. But then he'd swung back the other way, and then back again, first doubting one reaction and then another. Drifting in and out of sleep, however, the memory of the confrontation, the way Elisabeth Dunlop had aroused him, had been so powerful that his apprehension had dimmed and all but disappeared. But in the unfolding daylight his fantasies were beginning to look increasingly improbable as, in truth, he knew they must be. Still, he wasn't ready to discount the possibility that he had been in her thoughts too, maybe even in her dreams . . .

He increased his pace a little. A lizard fled from his path into the dull-brown scrub which grew on both sides of the road and spread for miles around. The knee-high grass rustled gently as other hidden reptiles and insects moved away from the human presence. Before long, he rounded the last corner which brought the perimeter fence and its large gates into view. There at the gate was Jocifar gesturing at him to hurry up.

'Hey, Good-Luck,' he whispershouted in Tonga, 'they've been calling for you! For the last fifteen minutes!' He tapped his watch face.

Good-Luck brushed past the watchman, briefly clasping his hand in his own, and saw that it was ten to seven – it was not so late. Through the other side, the brown of the road stood out against the lush green grass of the lawn, its even trim testimony to the constant sweep of the curved panga blade: from shoulder to shoulder and back again. The uniform green was occasionally interrupted by bright splurges of reds, yellows, blues: flowers burgeoning in plumped soil, collected in circular beds and rectangular beds, large and small beds. There were contoured bushes whose profiles betrayed hours of toil and full-canopied trees which provided large areas of shade. On one edge where the grass was stubbornly refusing to grow, a sprinkler arched lazily over and back.

At the kitchen door he paused, listening. Hearing nothing, he slipped inside on the balls of his feet, as soundlessly as possible, plucked the white coat from the back of the door and donned it in one smooth motion. The kettle, he saw, was already on the stove; the ring beneath it glowered red and accusing at him.

In the corridor, he knocked lightly on the heavy door and left the tray, retreating quickly.

He began to clear up what had been left from the previous evening – scraping, conserving, refrigerating and washing; his movements were practised, mechanical. Suddenly he heard a muffled sound – a laugh? – from behind the heavy door. There followed another, a little louder this time, less wary, and then another. He tried to ignore them, concentrating more on his task, but found he couldn't. They seemed almost to be directed at him. So much so that he listened a little closer, surprised to find they disturbed him. He realised he was jealous! Next he heard a low throaty chuckle which rose suddenly to a sharp cry but which was quickly stifled in Elisabeth Dunlop's throat as if by a sudden feeling of guilt. It was all so clear that he could virtually see her soundless convulsions as she tried to control herself, and he felt another stab of jealousy.

Then, all at once, the jealousy gave way to annoyance. She was laughing at *him!* They were both laughing at him. Another stifled cry heightened his paranoia until he found their intimacy almost unbearable. He felt ridiculous standing there, being made to listen, and he had a sudden and powerful impulse to drop everything and run ouside, to get as far away from them as possible.

But he suppressed the urge, leaning instead against the counter and staring out through the mosquito screens into the middle distance as he tried to regain control of his feelings. He knew he was being foolish, knew he was being irrational, but somehow the knowledge of it didn't help. After a time of just standing there, however, his anxiety began slowly to fade. Gradually, the image in front of him, the view from the kitchen window, came into focus, until at last the manicured garden lay pristine before him. Curiously, though he spent the major part of the day in this house, in this room actually, it was a picture he had never really looked at before. He saw it all as if with fresh eyes, as if it had been put there yesterday. It was a sight to behold: well-planned, beautifully executed; each bush, each flower, each blade of grass seemed to fill a certain space, to have a specific purpose. The splendour of it all brought the township – which had no greens, or yellows or reds, or trees or bushes even – suddenly and painfully to mind.

The juxtaposition in his mind jarred him; it shocked him. What on earth had he been thinking about? Making love with Mrs Dunlop? A white woman? Did he really think so? One black man comes to dinner and suddenly he's in bed with the boss's wife! Did he imagine also that he could sit and eat with the Dunlops, that he too could drink their wine and make jokes with them about their servant?

The idea of it, suddenly so ridiculous, his stupidity, all at once so transparent, made him laugh – quietly to himself at first, then a little louder, then more and more, until it was a thumping great self-derisory guffaw. Tears rolled down his cheeks. At the same time he began to shake his head fero-ciously as though to erase the whole of the previous evening from it, the whole unreal affair, which had made him think that Mrs Dunlop wanted to make love with him! He caught himself then and stopped, but soon he was laughing again, shaking his head again, this time in disbelief. He laughed and laughed and continued laughing, until he had laughed the man in the Mercedes right out of his system. Him and Mrs Dunlop? Indeed!

He took a deep breath then, let out a long sigh, wiped his eyes and set about his task with more vigour. He loaded the last of the saucepans into the sink and opened the hot water tap wide, filling the tub with suds, and when it was full he buried his hands up to his elbows in the liquid, and began to scrub hard. He heard another muffled sound from the bedroom, a low moan, and he chuckled, thinking how lucky he was to have caught himself in time.

Next, he began to make breakfast. He set the oil to heat on the stove, retrieved some eggs from the fridge, and just as he cracked the second one into the frying pan, he heard her enter the kitchen behind him. The door creaked as it swung open. Facing away from her, over the stove, he breathed a polite 'Good morning madam,' at the wall, but didn't turn. In spite of what he had so recently decided, he was nervous. He knew that she would be standing there with her dressing gown barely covering her, as she did every morning when she came down the hall to make sure that things were under way. Suddenly all his bravado deserted him, his thoughts were confused again. The memory of their encounter the previous evening flashed once again through his mind.

'What are you doing Good-Luck?' she asked suddenly, in a stern voice. Her tone caused him to turn in surprise, twisting his body at the waist. But his feet wouldn't respond, his legs were suddenly weak so he was off-balance, not quite round to face her.

'Madam?'

'What are you doing boy?'

'Making breakfast madam.' He saw that her hair was unkempt and her face still had some sleep-lines on it. He thought that he could detect the faint smell of recent love-making.

'What day is it Good-Luck?'

Then he remembered. Sunday. No breakfast until after church. The eggs popped and cracked in the hot oil behind him, underlining his mistake, but he held on, not turning – holding out, he didn't know why. Maybe something had changed after all.

'Shit man, the eggs are burning!' she shouted, and her eyes went over his shoulder to the clock, 'and by the way, you were late!' Then she turned on her heel and left, the door swinging open and shut in her wake.

Only now did he wheel round and recover the frying pan from the stove, relieved he supposed, wondering how he could have forgotten and whispering under his breath, 'Yes madam, Sunday. Breakfast after church madam, as always.'

August Braxton

Sermons in Stone

from *Full Things Spill*

Vlad sat in the open window, kicking his heels two hundred feet above the shoppers and spitting down upon them the glycerine gobs that he blew into life between his lips, freeing them to hang from fine threads stretching longer and longer until they snapped and the sputum sprang free to fall through space.

We were going on a day out, going for a drive to the caves arranged the week before. Vlad was on the lookout for Mister Anthony's car in the blue shadows below. He had sheared the head off a boil when shaving and tissue paper was stuck there now like a moth settled on the red bark of his cheek. He flicked cushions of moss free from the windowsill, bent almost double to fit in the frame. He had a griffin's head for heights, crouched against the leaf-green sky, his bony shoulders jagging his thin T-shirt. The mid-morning sun pulled the shadows of his swinging legs down the warming brickwork until they were six stories long and he could scissor them over the open windows beneath.

We heard the squeal of the horn at last, tinny and insistent and lost at once among all the other noises of the city. Summer makes so many calls to life, yelling them up through the canyon air with all its mouths, and this was just one more. But it was meant for us, for me and Vladimir. There was no hurry, it was delicious just to ignore and delay. Vlad slipped from one shirt to another, saying that nothing looked right. As he moulted each one and stood bare-chested, I caught the ozone smell his skin always gave off. His neck was a brindle of love-bites. The purple impress of teeth made me feel suddenly proud. On a whim, he decided we should take Madeline in a cardboard box. She had been sitting on the television all morning, endlessly licking her fur and scratching her fleabites, her tail swinging coyly across the screen, yet at Vlad's approach she bounded like a lithe black muscle through the skylight and onto the roof. She was no fool, Madeline.

We, in our turn, fled down twenty flights of stairs and out into the buttery light of the street where Mister Anthony stood jangling the car keys and waving blindly against the sun. He was a knot of excitement already unravelling. He looked about to burst. He had been at the casino all night and still wore a sharkskin jacket and cummerbund. He stood no bigger than the roof of the car, looking more squat than ever by daylight. He wore sunglasses with orange frames; Vlad said they made him look like an insect.

The car was long and low and powdery blue from a distance. Closer, the skin of paint was mangy and flushed with a rose coloured rash that spread across the bonnet. With the sun bouncing off its bodywork, it looked glamorous in the street, all calm and sleek. It was a de luxe model, a Corinthian, Vlad said. Its worth only encouraged him to drive it like a bumper car. Since he never could tolerate being life's passenger, Vlad was to drive and Mister Anthony to sit behind him and navigate, his chin resting on Vlad's shoulder. That way he could share his chauffeur's view, aligning himself with a squint to what he thought Vlad saw through the smeared film of the windscreen. But Vlad's eyes were bloodshot and pinned to nothing. I doubted he saw anything that his elderly friend would recognise.

'O Jesus, keep your eyes on the road,' he pleaded in a half hiss, gripping the back of Vlad's seat. 'If you have to drive then at least look . . .' But he never finished his warning because, with speechless ease, a motorcade rolled out in the street before us. Faster than a cortege, much faster, but just as quiet.

The old princess sat alone in the back of the largest car. It was lit as brightly as a shop window and she stared straight ahead like a mannequin behind clean glass. She was said to have a nervous twitch, to be palsied, to need transfusions of blood purer than her own. She had hair like smoothed fur. But she was gone again without a sound, a hectic tapestry of summer traffic pulled along in her breathless wake. Vlad had the window down at once and both hands cupped to his mouth.

'Off with her head, the mad bitch,' he yelled with reddened face. But she was far away, off to her palace or hospital, and only the sapphire flicker of darting police lights betrayed her trail. Mister Anthony's eyes had popped open with delight. He forgot to continue chastising Vlad.

Our next stop was to collect Mister Anthony's mother. She lived in a narrow house, boxed in by a sunflower that grew in the small front garden and raised a bullying head against her upstairs window. She was easily forgotten in its presence. Inside, there were no corners to the rooms where the walls met because cobwebs robbed the angles and, when a door closed, they wafted all at once like fraying looms of silk. She was smaller than her son; standing side by side they might have been hollow dolls made to nest inside each other. She said not a word but moved below and before us into the kitchen where we collected the picnic she had grouped around a thermos flask, while she silently filled a bag with tomatoes that she severed between thumbnail and forefinger from plants in the yard.

Vlad had recently had an incisor pulled and his mouth was dark and breath still heavy with the odour of stale blood. Next to him in the Corinthian sat Mamma Matrioshka, as we christened her, who would half turn her head at the sound of her son's girlish laughter, her hooknose in profile. Moles, like flecks of soot, were flicked across her powdered cheek. Mister Anthony sat next to me, always bent forward with his chin nestled against Vlad's neck, whorls of brilliantined hair scraped towards a bald patch that shone as pink as coral. His ears leaked an amber wax that seemed to seal the openings like the resin from a split stem. Every now and then Vlad brushed this giant head from his shoulder but it soon returned, a bone planet in orbit. And I sat next to him, wordsore and cactushanded from the previous afternoon. Both stung and stinging.

We rattled and swerved under Vlad's guidance towards open country, the weedy outskirts of town slipping by in wisps until we were suddenly between harvested fields where stacked and lonely bales of hay stood like wardrobes among the stubble. A tented sky sagged overhead, hot and dull as canvas, the light through it filtered and lifeless. Before long we left all traffic behind and pursued our course alone along a motorway stretching as smooth as moleskin from the windscreen to the horizon. Vlad steered with his elbows while he moulded his quiff afresh, the wind rushing in through the open windows to fill our mouths and blow ash from my cigarette into Matrioshka's hair. It was Mister Anthony who first saw the solitary bird that followed the car as if on a string. It had the distinctive markings of some species, but none of us knew which. Mister Anthony said kites looked like that, or even eagles. Then Vlad leant out of the window to have a look, while the car, jumping at the chance to take on a life of its own, snaked out of control and off the road. It was a vulture for sure, Vlad shouted, his head craned to the open sky, the pearls of sweat drying on his exposed neck.

'Come inside at once. Christ, Vlad. Please,' pleaded Mister Anthony through hands that had flown to his face and were hinged together like a book. He peeped at me through a chink in its spine then back to his lover. But Vladimir, eternally heroic catamite that he was, had us back on the road again and on our way to the caves. Vlad the Inhaler. If anything, the bird was an albatross to navigate by.

The field that the car had swerved into was a charred expanse of burnt earth smeared like boneblack against a pale horizon. In the last seconds of the car's freedom, the quickening smell of arson made me catch my breath and remember home. Mister Anthony's peevish scolding of Vlad, in his breathless foreign accent, brought me back to his side as the first signpost announcing the caves appeared. Matrioshka still sat staring straight ahead, her long ear lobes trembling like wattles with each bump in the road, the picnic bag giant in her lap. Perhaps she was deaf, or mute. She certainly knew how to sit still, unlike her fidgeting son.

The prairie flatness ended with a smashed chain of hills and there, among a great tumble of crepe paper rock, was the yawning mouth of a cave. It was open wide and full of saplings, hart's-tongue fern shivering along its lip, the jowls splashed with mustard yellow lichen. A small shed stood near the entrance and we paid our money to an indifferent woman who peeled potatoes into an orange bowl. Our bird still wheeled overhead as we gripped the groaning guide-rope and slid under the earth's crust to squeeze between its skin and bone.

The passage was clammy and cut stone steps overran with a reddened water, thick and rich in mineral dyes. The walls were sticky with a kind of phlegm. I led the way, not knowing where, whilst Vlad brought up the rear. He shouted into the dark and the walls shouted back with lungs of their own and mouths thickened with rock. He clapped his hands to the hollow's applause. It was warmer in the passage than it was outside, a heavy mammalian heat that felt like a fever after the cool draught of the journey. Mister Anthony wheezed behind me, his breath breaking in gusts against my back as he rolled bow-leggedly from step to step. Behind him, his mother's progress was lost among the splashed footsteps. There was no other noise. We were blind but for the occasional light bulb losing its power to shine through a thick cast of condensation, beads of water clinging like warts to the glass. Blind, and all but silent.

Full things spill, of course. That is their fate. Things are brimful one minute and empty the next, their contents spilled forth to soak through thirsty soils. And then things fill again like cisterns, like hearts. Bursting then burst. But drop by drop. Pitter patter pitter patter, drip by drop towards emptiness.

The coarse light in the first cave exposed cold agates among the folds of rock, dull and smooth as kidneys in the quarried flanks of a carcass. High above them, forming the roof, a sagging canopy of solid calcium leaked in a million places, as honeycombed as tripe. With the unfolding clamour of wings, Mister Anthony's umbrella was suddenly alive. He held it at arm's length and on tiptoe above our heads. The drops drummed heavily against its taut skin and, in the huddle below, Matrioshka was muffled against us, leaving the picnic bag standing alone and exposed to the internal rain.

Stalagmites strained towards stalactites as we shuffled downward. Sometimes they met to form a veined and slender column, but more often they just poked urgently toward an intended conjunction that would only be gained drop by salty drop. These were the teats of the world, lactating endless milk. Warning signs said that the slightest touch would snap the results of an eternity's suckling; between them, the spokes of the blundering umbrella sent a xylophone's worth crashing to our feet, a confusion of wax fingers pointing scoldingly at what might have been. Vlad put the sharpest in his pocket and kicked the others aside. Unstaunchable, the wet nurse leaked over her wounds in our wake.

Across the black and thick-skinned water of an underground lake a frozen cascade of crystal descended massively to meet its own reflection, glittering like vomitted ice. The afternoon above our heads could never have been this warm. The smell from the coloured spotlights, of hot metal and dusty flex, made this cave the snuggest. No one knew the depth of the lake or how far it extended through flooded chambers; it had never been explored. Deep down, catadromous fish, so transparent that flukes could be seen in their guts, dragged whiskery barbels through depths unchallenged by frogmen, bubbles hatching from their glass-blowers lips.

We climbed into a waiting boat that was tethered to a spur of rock and cast off, the dim shore slipping from sight. Ahead of us, in their coracle, a father rowed identical twins toward the further shore. He steered skilfully, while they trailed listless fingers through the green-lit ripples, gliding soundlessly as swans, their thin girlish arms scabbed with splashes of mud. Our boat rocked terribly in contrast. Vlad and Mister Anthony each had an oar and sat facing Matrioshka and I. We seemed to sail through our own tempest. Vlad was intent on skimming the water's surface with his oar, creating furrows that swirled with the paintbox colours of overhead lights, and drenching the crew. In return, the reflected ripples gently lapped the jagged roof. As for Mister Anthony, his leg had gone to sleep and, as he rubbed the blood back into circulation, his idle oar slipped its rollocks to float alligator-like just out of reach of our spiralling course. He still wore his sunglasses and each lens mirrored a tiny grotto where every light shone with pinprick precision and his mother and I loomed convexly. As the boat wobbled us from one light-effect to the next, so the sockets of shadow behind them lengthened down his cheeks. With his bursting cummerbund and white shirt, he looked like a panda adrift.

The oar's retrieval necessitated the histrionic flailing of Vlad's arms across the abyss and we gripped his legs as he leant overboard, our own sniggering figurehead. His efforts at capsizal almost worked; we pulled him back just in time, a string of rosary beads alone lost in the struggle. The boat steadied again, it was time for Mister Anthony to take the photographs. The camera's mercurial flash drenched the cave, the lard and tallow and glue that everywhere hung and flowed momentarily solidifying in its glare. Limestone shone, slumped and viscous in the earth's maw. And again, the innards twitching each time we yelled 'Cheese!' and the cave's rubber musculature flexing with the echo. Then, among all the ribbons of noise, Mamma Matrioshka started bubbling with sound, gently at first but growing louder. She was murmuring, in her own indistinct tongue, something urgent and broken. She was terrified. The last flash betrayed her frantically crossing herself with shadow, a crucifix swinging madly from a chain around her wrist. We headed at once for the shore, her sobs drowned by the splashing of oars.

Climbing back up the stone steps, we approached the raw sheet of light at the mouth of the cave. Slurred birdsong filled its larynx. The strain of so much sky yanked twitching retinas back into focus as we blinked our way out of a green and gold night that smelled of scorched linen, and into the jabbering confusions of August. In the half-light I stopped to smooth my hair and wipe my mouth. Vlad's kiss, back in the dark, had tasted of endings; it had been sharp enough and full enough. In reality, his body was so slight it always shocked me. He had the bones of a bird. Grafting together, he pushed us against the passage wall. Our mouths found each other at once. Milky water gurgled over calciferous lips in the chambers behind us. His tongue was smoke-soured and his neck wet and it seemed for a second as if a shock jumped between our breastbones, jolting from one to the other and back again. The bifurcations of stalactite and prick rose up my belly and down my leg like the arms of a clock. It was somehow time, they said stiffly. We kissed more earnestly still, wrapping tongues and grinding foreheads. We were only bone and gristle and teeth and hair;

they were no obstacle to us. But time was running out.

Where cave people once blundered blindly, Vlad struck a light, his fingers albinotic in the bobbing flame. He carved a faltering heart in the wall with his knife in raw, prehistoric scratches. There was just time to add our initials before we raced upwards to join mother and son, the stone's opened pores bleeding in the silence.

Of course the passing around of sandwiches and the un-wrapping of tinfoil held its own ineluctable drama as we ate our picnic up near the crest of the hill. The ritual helped as-sauge Matrioshka's panic and the cave's hollow enormity, way down below our rug, was soon forgotten. The sandwiches were squashed and soggy with lake water and the tea from the flask tasted of soup. We were privy no longer to the sole sound of each others' breath, for a wind blew down from the hill and shook frilly birches until they shivered and unseen sheep bleated in dismay among the gorse, tufts of wool drifting free of thorns to turn cartwheels over the heather. A cinnabar moth, or some kind of moth, settled on the rug, its wings spread in the sun. Near it, the bag of cherry tomatoes smelled sweetly antiseptic. It was good just to eat; the four of us sat nearer the sky than usual, shoes off and toes curled among the grass, in comfortable extremity. Unbelievably, perhaps, our bird still circled and waited.

'Vladimir, you're bloody disgusting,' cried Mister An-thony rolling his giant head around to face me, as if for help. Vlad sat with his widest leer, pushing a sausage of chewed sandwich through the new gap in his teeth. As if from a nose-bleed, the liquid from the cave had smeared and dried across his face, bright as cochineal

'Naturally, your majesty, I aim to please,' Vlad fawned. 'Perhaps the readies could be coughed up for a nice gold crown? That is, if it pleases my sovereign liege.' And with that Vlad poked Mister Anthony in his side with a cattleprod finger until he screamed with delight and rolled into a squirming ball at Vlad's feet. His mother, by now immune to antic sport, brushed the crumbs from her skirt and stared stonily down on the plain of England, her coat, stretched over a boulder to dry, the ensanguined evidence of a lost afternoon. Soon he slept, his barrel chest resounding with snores, leaving Vlad free to arrange an artful web of burrs across his back, with no thought of symmetry, in an approximation of a dartboard which he drowsily pelted with sheep dung until he scored a bull's-eye.

We had to drive as quickly as possible. There were no working lights on the car other than the dragon-red ones burning softly in the tail fins and darkness would soon sweep across the land. It was in the sky already, strands of it like windborne ash sullying the clouds. Faster and faster, we drove back through the hollow landscape with its legion shadows spilling in our path. The day was deflating and a harvest moon was already in place as its orange and open-mouthed puncture. But there was still light left and the sun had yet to set. We still had time. It was Matrioshka herself who pointed through the open window to the sky where there hung, perfectly becalmed, a school of hot-air balloons. They were giants, even in the distance, and trailed ropes that swung a thousand feet up. We drove through their five grey shadows, the windscreen, between each one, catching the glare of the sun and glowing like yellow cellophane.

There was an ice cream van pulled up in a lay-by nearer the city and we stopped to buy ourselves cones. The van was almost hidden by the lower boughs of chestnut trees leaning into the road and watery pink light wove down through the black rigging of leaves in luminous, shifting pools. A group of children were gathered around the window, a clutter of small hands holding money to the vendor. Their faces were flushed and burnt, as if the sky had sifted down as dust to redden them, and their hair was thick with spores. Above us all, a vapour trail, sinuous through a ruined sky, was breaking and dissolving in a string of ghost words, too far away to read. They seemed to speak of the end of the world in wisps and tatters. I carried our ice creams back to the others, two cones in each hand, as headlights swivelled out from the road. Each car, each lorry passed by with a whoosh and sigh of tyres. The day was almost over now and the caves left far behind. The lights of Pleasure Island lay someway ahead; hypnotic, radar bright, meaningless and beautiful. By the time we closed ourselves into the warm insides of the car it was dusk and we licked the white peaks in darkness.

Jane Harris

Vantage

To David, best wishes from Jane x.

Tom didn't want to go to the Caledonia House Hotel. It was Mother's Day, Fay's mother was up and their daughter Lorna was over for the weekend. Normally, Tom might have chosen somewhere more tasteful for lunch, perhaps in the West End. But Fay had already booked.

'They serve plain food,' she said. 'And that's all Gran will eat. End of story.'

She settled into the back seat with Lorna and Gran sat in front with Tom, where Fay said there was more legroom.

'Snug as four bugs in a rug,' said Gran, fumbling with the seatbelt clasp.

'Hardly mummy,' said Fay. 'This car is celebrated for its roominess. Four peas in a pod more like.'

'Four what?'

'Peas in a pod mother!'

'No need to shout, I'm not deaf.'

The display on the dashboard read one o'clock, which was cutting it fine because the table was booked for one-thirty. Fay said she hoped however, that her husband would not be doing his Jackie Stewart. She showed Lorna the ring he'd given her for her birthday and insisted on wearing the scarf Lorna had brought over from Edinburgh, even though it didn't match her outfit. Fay had given her own mother an embroidered blouse and a jacket.

'You've not to spend so much,' Gran had said when she opened the parcels. 'There's no need.'

'Catch a grip mum,' said Fay. 'It's not often we're all together. Besides. We can afford it.'

The car sucked up the miles of suburban tarmac. Tom gazed over the steering wheel. At the edge of the city, he put his foot down and took pleasure in pressing the car into each curve of the country road. Lorna rested her head against the window with her eyes closed. Fay pointed out interesting details of the scenery: the Queen's View; a coffee shop she particularly liked; the shambles left behind by some travelling people; and the house where Billy Connolly used to live. She grasped the hand-strap on the ceiling and every time Tom took a corner she made a sharp noise by sucking air through her teeth. She exclaimed aloud whenever they passed a field of lambs.

'Now after lunch we're going for a walk in the hotel gardens,' she said. 'Because there is the most superb, superb view of Loch Lomond.'

Gran didn't say much. Any time she did try to start a conversation, Fay said 'Uh-huh, mm-hmm,' and changed the subject to something less boring, or drew their attention to the landscape. At one point, Gran mentioned a man she'd read about in the paper.

'You went out with him once, Fay.'

'Nonsense. I never went out with anyone called Spencer mother. Ever.'

'Yes you did. He used to drive a Morris. Anyway, he's turned out a millionaire.'

'Och for pete's sake, *Spencer*,' said Fay, pronouncing the name in a way that suggested she now remembered everything. 'Tiny Spencer. A millionaire? Och, exactly the sort of person I went out with. Hoo-hoo-hooo, old Tiny.' And every so often, Fay chuckled again, as if savouring moments she and this Spencer had shared.

By the time they arrived at the hotel, the car-park was full.

'We'll get out here and you find somewhere to put the car, Tom,' said Fay. 'It's nearly half past.'

'Perfect,' said Tom. He dropped them at the door and spun the wheel sharply as he accelerated, sending up a spray of gravel chips. Luckily, none landed anywhere near Fay or her mother.

Inside, the women headed for the corner of a blue plaid lounge. Fay peered out onto the roof of an extension. 'You'd think they'd put some tubs down there or something,' she said in a loud voice, adding a phrase she'd learned at her nightclass. *'C'est terrible.'*

A barman with mottled cheeks took their drinks order. Fay couldn't decide what to drink at all until Tom arrived and asked for tomato juice. Then she slammed the drinks list down on the table and said well, that was exactly what she'd have too.

'I don't feel like anything alcoholic at all somehow. Not even a Campari.' She looked brightly round at her family. Everyone smiled and blinked back at her. Then she picked up the menu and started reading aloud everything that was printed on it. When she'd finished she said there must be something wrong with her tummy because the only thing that appealed to her was the plate of assorted cold cuts with chef salad, baked potato and choice of three dressings.

'Och look! Dr. Hamilton-Menzies and her mum!' Fay pointed out a woman in her mid-forties sitting on a couch with an elderly lady and a small girl in dungarees. The women were well-groomed and the twin tilt of their noses indicated they were related. They were deep in conversation, half-turned towards each other over the head of the child, their knees almost touching. The older woman was stroking the child's hair.

'Smashing day for it doctor!'

The doctor narrowed her eyes in Fay's direction, nodded briefly then pulled her daughter onto her knee, cuddling her closer. Fay stared at the group on the couch then turned quickly to the window. She sniffed. 'It would have been wonderful if one of you had been a doctor.'

Lorna began shredding her beermat into pellets and flicking them against the ashtray.

Tom scowled at her. 'Act your age.'

The head waiter arrived, looking hungover. He apologised: there was no sole left. 'Would sir and the ladies care for a piece of salmon done in a similar sauce?'

Tom said no, he wouldn't care for that in the least, and frowned into the menu again.

'Salmon's fine,' said Lorna.

'Yes, very nice,' said Gran.

Tom snapped the menu shut. 'I'll have the roast beef,' he said. 'But only,' he raised his forefinger and threatened the employee with it, 'only if the meat's nicely pink. A good piece of pink beef.' He spoke at a speed that suggested he considered the man to be either deaf or stupid.

'Understood sir. Absolutely,' said the waiter, ducking his head and rushing towards the toilets.

'Look look look, over there,' hissed Fay. 'Angus whojemaflick from STV. With the toupee.'

'Oh aye,' said Tom. He rolled his eyes skywards: it took more than a minor sports commentator to impress him.

Gran tutted. 'You and your television Fay.'

Fay set her jaw and scowled at her mother. 'I might just order an aperitif after all.'

Everyone stared down at the shiny tartan carpet.

Tom took his time choosing what the ladies would drink with their meal. Naturally, he'd only be having mineral water because of the car. Fay rattled the ice in her spritzer impatiently.

'The Sancerre,' said Tom finally to the wine steward.

'Very good sir. That'll be the red Sancerre?'

'Red? Have you no white?'

'No, sorry sir. Only the red.'

'How unusual that you should have a red and no white San-

cerre.' Tom made a face as if that was exactly the sort of cir-
cumstance he'd expect at the Caledonia House Hotel.

'What about the . . . the Muscadet, sir?'

Fay pretended to be sick at the mere mention of Muscadet.
'No, no, no, no, no.'

'Pouilly Fuisse?' suggested Lorna.

'Not listed,' said Tom.

'Have they any of that Liebfrau Milk?' said Gran. 'We always have that at Jack and Betty's.' But no-one seemed to
notice she'd spoken.

Tom re-examined each page of the list slowly. Fay glared
out of the window, pushing air through her lips in bursts. Her
nails rattled against the dark varnish of the table like arrows on
a breastplate.

'The Chablis,' said Tom eventually, passing the wine list
over his shoulder. Fay slugged back the remains of her drink
and waggled her glass.

They moved through to the dining room. It was extremely
busy. A young man did something complicated with cutlery at
their table. After a few moments Fay and Lorna had to swap
places because people whizzed right by Fay's chair every two
seconds and it was making her head worse. Someone offered
them bread rolls from a basket and then the starters arrived.
Tom was pleased to note he'd been correct about the seafood
being swamped in a ghastly Marie Rose sauce. When Fay
helped everyone to more wine, his nostrils flared like there was
a sudden bad smell at the table.

They discussed child abuse. Fay told Tom he didn't know
what these people did to their children. Tom suggested there
was no need to raise her voice since he could hear perfectly
well, and that he thought social workers dragging kids off in
the middle of the night smacked of a barbarism that was posi-
tively mediaeval. Fay said quite obviously there was no point
in talking about it and shoved her plate aside. She took a gulp

from her glass and lit a cigarette.

'Such a dreadful thing,' said Lorna.

'Oh aye.' Tom turned on her. 'No doubt with your vast worldly experience you'd have it sorted out in seconds.' He smirked. 'Never mind the lawyers and the social work department, they should consult a typist.' He and Fay exchanged a look and chuckled quietly. Lorna gouged a chunk out of the butter and began knifing it into her roll.

'It's Satanist,' said Gran, who'd silently demolished a goblet of prawns. 'Satanic. They say . . .'

'Uh-huh, mm-hmm. Not always mummy,' said Fay, then shouted: 'Och look over there everyone at that adorable wee girl with the flowers.'

At tables throughout the dining room, heads turned. Several people stared at Fay. But she didn't seem to notice. Her fingers worked nervously as she gazed towards the window-table. Dr. Hamilton-Menzies' little daughter was offering a cluster of snowdrops to her grandmother; the doctor was laughing and hauling up the straps on the toddler's dungarees; and a man with snowy hair who'd joined them, sat with his back towards Fay and family, his shoulders shaking with laughter at something the doctor had said.

'Lovely thought,' said Fay. She sucked in her cheeks, drew her head back to focus on the bottle, and topped up her wine-glass. Tom opened his mouth to say something, then changed his mind. Instead, he pressed his lips together and began blowing air through them, making the noise of a horse. Fortunately a boy arrived brandishing knives.

'Who has the sole?' he asked. Tom gestured to Lorna and Gran and then at his own setting.

'Hang on,' said Lorna. 'It's salmon, not sole.'

Tom laughed. 'Unless sole's on again.'

'Yes, of course sir. My mistake,' said the boy, who looked as though he might have been in the company of the head waiter the previous evening. 'Salmon'. He laid fish knives for Lorna, Tom and Gran, then disappeared.

'Aren't you having beef, dad?'

'Of course,' said Tom quietly. 'Beef.' He raised his hands and pressed his fingertips to his eyes. 'Beef,' he said again. 'Beef.'

Fay ground her cigarette into the ashtray. She didn't say anything but her entire figure suggested satisfaction at Tom's mistake. She emptied the dregs of the wine into Gran's glass.

'Order another bottle, Lorna,' said Tom quietly. With a scowl at Fay, he produced a diary and began leafing through the pages. Gran looked at him fondly.

'Never stops working, does he?'

'That's for fucking sure,' said Fay through clenched teeth. A greyish fleck of her spittle described a neat arc over the table and landed in her daughter's glass.

The salmon turned up, stuffed with prawns and oozing lobster sauce. The beef arrived in a dark gravy, redolent of school dinners, the meat the colour of old leather. Fay said she wasn't at all surprised. Gran couldn't see what was wrong with it. Tom probed the flesh with the tip of his knife.

'Send it back dear,' said Fay, attacking a platter of tongue and what could have been a whole shredded cabbage.

'Thank you my sweet, I am quite capable of complaining myself.' Tom summoned the head waiter and, without a word, indicated his plate. The waiter raised one eyebrow and charged instantly into the kitchens. It was evident that he and Tom belonged to some secret gentleman's society with its own code system.

'I always do the complaining when we're in France,' said Fay. 'Tom can't cope with the language, can you dear?' Tom was about to defend himself when the headwaiter returned. It seemed all the beef had been cooked to the same degree. Naturally, there'd be no charge.

'Just make some nominal reduction.' Tom dismissed the man with two flicks of his hand.

'Well negotiated, dad.'

'Uh-huh, mm-hmm,' said Fay. '*I'm* the one does all the complaining in France.'

While they ate, Fay described amusing things that had happened to them in French hotels. She and Tom couldn't agree on the exact location of one *auberge* with particularly eccentric staff. 'We'll look it up in the Michelin when we get home,' said Fay. 'No doubt we'll find it was the Bellecote in Savoie as I've maintained from the beginning.'

Somehow, no-one had any appetite for dessert. Lorna had wolfed her meal and was investigating the gardens, so Fay ordered coffee for three. 'And I'll have mmm . . . oh, an Armagnac.'

Tom curled his lip and she turned on him, her intonation suddenly sinister. '*I'm* the mother here. *My* day. I have what I want.'

Tom said nothing until the waiter had gone, then he sighed.

'It would have been nice to have coffee in the lounge dear.'

'I think you'll find the lounge is full dear,' Fay explained. 'Otherwise the waiter would have suggested it.'

'Do you think so dear?'

'Yes. He'd have suggested they serve coffee in the lounge.'

'You're convinced of that then?' said Tom, his tone expressionless.

'*Mais certainement*. They do that if the lounge is full. They make you have coffee at your table.'

'Miss.' Tom hailed a passing waitress. He spoke in a tired voice. 'Would it be possible to have coffee in the lounge please?'

'I'm afraid the lounge is full, sir,' said the waitress, hurrying away.

Fay sat back in her chair and lit another cigarette. She tilted her head and blew a lot of smoke up in the air. Then she stretched her arm out into the aisle to see what her fingernails looked like from a distance. Tom chewed at the inside of his cheek, glaring at her, then excused himself from the table. Presently, Fay turned to her mother.

'See the brooch I bought, mum? Rennie Mac.' She held her jacket by its lapel and allowed her mother to examine the brooch.

'Very nice.'

'D'you like it?' Fay was still holding the jacket.

'Pardon?'

'Do you like it?'

'Yes. Very nice.'

'Seventy pounds.' Fay dropped her lapel into place. Gran gasped.

'You take me aback sometimes Fay. You really do.'

Fay beamed out of the window, swinging her leg and puffing at her cigarette. Gran glowered down at the embroidery on her blouse until Tom came back from the gent's, and then she frowned across at him. Lorna breezed in, seconds later.

'Hello dear!' Fay called out so the other diners could overhear her family's chatter. 'Where have you been then?'

'Putting a tampon in mum.'

'Oh! Uh-huh, mm-hmm. I watched a superb programme yesterday about Gielgud. Marvellous. Of course, he was deeply, deeply homosexual. You'd have enjoyed it dear.'

There was a moment of quiet, then Gran spoke in a low, clear voice. 'You waste yourself.'

'What? What did you say?'

'Sitting all day watching videos. Rubbish. Wasting what's left of your life.'

Fay's mouth worked in silence for a second. Her fingers fluttered nervously on the tablecloth, then tightened into fists as her features crumbled in on themselves. She burst into tears.

'How dare you how dare you how dare you,' she moaned. Over and over.

'Perfect,' said Tom.

Everyone stared down at the remains of the meal.

Conversation faltered at adjoining tables. Fay appeared to have no strength left. Her head lolled forward onto her chest as she sobbed; her shoulders heaved. No-one said anything. Then there was the sound of movement from the other side of the room as people at the doctor's table made ready to leave.

Fay lifted her mascara-streaked face and sighed. For some apparently arbitrary reason of prestige, the doctor's party *would* be allowed to take coffee in the lounge. She pursed her lips. The man with snowy hair pushed back his chair and turned to survey the restaurant. At once, Gran's jaw dropped open, with such a crack she almost lost her top set.

'Alexander Spencer!'

Fay sniffed. 'What mother? What you on about now?'

'That's him Fay. Spencer. The millionaire.'

'Och for pete's sake don't be daft mummy. What would he be . . .' Fay's voice trailed off as she peered across the room. The man was in his sixties, with the craggy tan features that look most at home on a yacht. Normally, Fay would have noticed he was rather casually dressed for lunch in a hotel, with jeans and sweatshirt. But as it was, she was too flabbergasted. As it was, she was back with a jolt in May 1959: a drunken evening; the rear seat of a Morris; her legs splayed, her arms waving in the air, conducting; her head banging time on the ashtray.

'Tiny Spencer!' she gasped and with a shiver, imagined all over again the eager jab inflicted by the origin of Tiny's nickname; remembered how on the dance floor he'd tugged back his cuff and deposited a neat stream of Talisker-scented vomit up the sleeve of his dinner-jacket, thus not to desert her in the middle of a Gay Gordons. Later, she'd passed out in the back seat of the Morris and when she awoke neither Spencer, nor her knickers, were to be found.

Lorna and Tom were watching Fay with interest.

'That him right enough mum?'

'Watch what you're doing with your coffee dear.'

Gran tugged Fay's sleeve, loath to miss this opportunity of meeting a handsome millionaire. She'd never been averse to the odd flirtation and Spencer was what she'd called in 1959, 'swave'.

'Speak to him when he goes past Fay.'

'No mummy I will not.'

'Speak to him.'

'No! Catch a grip.'

'For dear sake here he's coming. Will you speak to him?'

The Hamilton-Menzies' path would bring him right past the table. In seconds, they'd be in the lounge, the opportunity of hailing Spencer casually and chatting for a moment, missed.

'Mr Spencer!'

The man paused and glanced down with a polite smile. His teeth were so white they were almost translucent and there looked to be too many of them for his mouth.

'Yes?'

'I believe you're an old friend of my mum's.' Lorna nodded in thinly disguised delight at Fay, who looked back at her through slitted eyes.

Spencer shifted his gaze to incorporate the others at the table. Facing the nondescript girl was an old woman in a chintzy blouse, twitching and twisting a napkin in her lap. The only man in the party was smartly dressed, but obviously trying to hide behind his hand, picking vaguely at his nose. He looked as though he wished he were somewhere else. The middle-aged woman opposite was familiar. She was smiling desperately at Spencer. Make-up coated the down on her chin and she wore a shiny blouse with a dark stain on the front. Her thin chiffon scarf clashed with her blouse and exaggerated the turkey-flesh of her throat. She looked as if she'd been crying. Spencer couldn't place her until she lifted a liqueur glass to her mouth and swallowed nervously. It was the way she drew back her lips from her teeth and made a smacking sound with her tongue that reminded him.

'Fay,' he said. 'Sweet Fay MacKenzie.' And the rest of the old rhyme popped automatically into his head, '*the finest ride in Lenzie*'. But he made sure not to say it.

'MacKenzie no more, Alexander,' scolded Fay. She sniffed, recovering herself. 'This is my husband Tom, Tom Cameron.' Tom leapt to his feet and pumped Spencer's hand, until he realised that Spencer was a good deal taller than himself, and quickly leaned against his chair so the difference in their heights was less noticeable. Fay spat out her remaining introductions like they were a couple of poisoned darts. 'My daughter, Lorna.' Spencer clicked his heels and nodded. 'And I'm sure you'll remember my mother, Agnes.'

'I'm eighty-six this year.' Gran grabbed Spencer's hand and wrinkled her nose flirtatiously.

No change there then, thought Spencer, remembering an unfortunate ten minutes in the woman's front room one evening while Fay was upstairs changing. He pressed Gran's hand, patted it and returned it to her lap, where it twitched and buried itself once more in her napkin. 'Well,' he said. His accent, once Midlothian, now hovered mid-Atlantic. 'How's life treating Fay?'

'Oh . . .' Fay waved her hand expansively, overturning a wineglass. Luckily there was only a dribble left in the bottom. She picked up a serviette and folded it carefully in squares. She shoved the glass to one side. Then she sponged at the stain.

It all seemed to take a long time.

'Marvellous,' she said. 'Absolutely smashing. But you know me Alexander, always did land on my feet. Yourself?'

'Fine. Yuh. Easier as we get older I find.'

'How right you are Alexander. How right you are.'

'Are you . . . forgive me. A personal question up here these days. Are you working?'

'Me? No, no, no, no. Eh, Tom's . . .'

'I've my own business. There's no real need for Fay to work.' Tom tilted his head and looked at Spencer steadily, along his nose. 'She has trouble with her back. Spencer nodded several times. He was looking at Fay. There was a little crease of concern between his brows.

'Yuh. Of course.'

'Tom's being modest. He's doing so well, aren't you dear? Working all over the place.'

'Right. Sure Tom. You're selling . . . ?'

'Och, not a salesman Alexander. For pete's sake. A businessman.'

Tom cleared his throat. 'Cranes.'

'Right. Sure. Enjoy it?'

'Eh . . . aye. There's cash in cranes. Recession allowed of course.' Tom chuckled and chaffed his hands together.

'Sure. Anyway . . .' Spencer was peering towards the lounge as if he wasn't particularly interested in Tom or in anything he might say. Then Gran slapped her hand on the table making everyone jump.

'I saw you in the paper Mister Alexander Spencer.'

'Shh. Mummy.'

'You used to come round in your car and take my daughter to the dancing. And now you're worth a mint.'

'Hoo-hoo-hooo!' Fay tapped the side of her head to show Spencer that her mother was practically senile. 'Is it not time you went to the toilet mum?'

Spencer smiled at Gran. 'You're so right Agnes. Yuh. Funny what happens.'

'Isn't it just Alexander. Isn't it just?'

There was an awkward silence. Spencer glanced at his watch and Tom noticed with a flash of envy that it was a Tag Heuer. He bit the inside of his cheek.

'Anyway. Yuh. Nice to bump into you again Fay.' Spencer held his hand out to Tom. 'Nice to meet you Tom.'

Tom took a deep breath and, to everyone's surprise, ignored the hand and stepped behind Fay's chair. He thrust his chin out at Spencer.

'Fay's thinking of going back on the boards you know.'

'. . . Well.' Spencer appeared lost for words.

'Yes. There's a BBC producer we know that's interested in her.' Tom touched Fay's shoulder and grinned down at her. He could feel the warmth of her skin through her blouse and noticed, for the first time in years, the baby-blond hairs on her neck.

'Yuh?' Spencer frowned. 'She had . . . well, still has, a talent. Sure.' He took a step backwards.

Fay wondered what talent it could be that Tiny thought he was talking about. He'd never seen her on the stage. She hesitated a moment, then placed her hand on Tom's. As she shifted in her seat, Tom's nostrils filled with her scent. It was the one he'd given her for Christmas. He remembered she'd wept on opening the package, because the bottle was such a beautiful shape. Just sat there, in her dressing gown, with a twist of tinsel in her hair, the tears streaming down her face.

'Oh aye. And she's a great wee mum too,' said Tom. 'Lorna there's thinking about going to college soon. Get some qualifications. Aren't you Lorna?'

Lorna nodded vigorously. 'Yes. Soon.'

'Never too late these days,' continued Tom.

'Yuh. Great.' Spencer glanced towards the door again and

his frown cleared. 'Oh, there's Jean looking for me.'

Fay breathed in noisily through her nose and announced: 'Dr. Hamilton-Menzies works at our local health centre. Talk about coincidence.'

Spencer nodded. He stared past their table as if he was trying to remember something. Then he blinked. 'She and I are old friends of course,' he said. 'Met at one of those May Balls in the late fifties. She was a youngster then of course.'

'Uh-huh, mm-hmm. Good good good.'

'Anyway. Must go. You take care now.'

Spencer dipped his head. He stepped carefully across the dining room, lifting his feet as though trying to keep his trouser-hems out of mud, and joined the doctor in the doorway. They exchanged a few words, then moved into the lounge. Neither looked back.

'My goodness,' said Fay. She blinked around brightly at her family.

After Tom paid, they went for a stroll in the hotel grounds, taking it easy at first because of the grandmother's leg and Fay's back and stilettos. They turned up a tarmac path, lined with rhododendrons and other plants, because Fay said there was a lovely view of Loch Lomond at the end. She and Tom walked arm in arm, leaning into the slope together; Lorna supported Gran. Fay paused at all the plants that had been labelled and read out the Latin names in a clear voice so everyone would know what they were, until Lorna got fed up and barged past with Gran. Tom jostled with her, dragging Fay by the elbow, and then they pretended to have a race, tottering along the tarmac in pairs.

'Oh Jesus!' panted Tom to Lorna as they neared the picnic-spot at the end, 'I've got the cripple!' and everyone laughed. They moved to the fence to get the benefit of the view and Fay, taking one look, spoke quickly:

'Och of course I was here in summer. There were no clouds

then.'

Below them, pine trees sloped into a milky fog and re-emerged some miles distant. They could just make out a dark edge where the forest met the waters of the loch. Above this line, a handful of islands with lush vegetation drifted in a pale blue mist.

Lorna chuckled dryly and put on her sarcastic voice. 'Oh, superb view.'

'Woopsydaisy,' said Gran. 'Fog.'

'*Mais, pas possible*,' said Fay, disowning the landscape. 'Can't see a damn thing.' She turned and started down the path on tippytoe.

'I'm sure it's lovely on a clear day dear,' said Tom, smiling innocently at her departing backside. On the way down to the car, they noticed several other families heading for the same vantage point, and Lorna sniggered to herself, about how no-one warned them to turn around, to save themselves the journey; that there was nothing to be seen because of the mist.

Karin Hurst

This Place

When Ligsy turned up, I thought, I'll murder Cayne. He stood on the doorstep, it was pouring rain, he was shivering.

'Come in then, if you're going to,' I said, which was a bit harsh I know, seeing's it wasn't his fault.

Ligsy had pink lines under his eyes as if he'd been crying, or was ill, and he had a long colourless dribble coming out of his nose, which he wiped on his sleeve when he saw me looking at it.

'Thanks Wen,' he said, and kind of loped in, ducking his head as if I was something important, and he pushed open the door of the sitting room.

Sheena and Paula were playing on the floor, so he had to tip-toe his way across the room to the settee. Even so, he trod on a bit of Lego and I heard it crack under his DMs. He sat on the edge of the settee and blew on his knuckles. He seemed to re-member his woolly hat then, and he pulled it off and smiled with half his mouth, embarrassed, then ruffled the back of his head. His hair looked as if someone had hacked it about with a blunt pair of scissors.

Sheena and Paula didn't look up, they're used to people coming and going, and they've seen Ligsy a few times. They carried on with their game, now the teacher's voice, now Cayne's voice, them wobbling the dolly when it was supposed to be doing the talking.

'Cayne said to come,' Ligsy said. 'It wouldn't be for long.'

'Cup of tea?' I asked him. 'Lemonade you two?' and went into the kitchen.

While I waited for the kettle, I thought about my dream again. You know how sometimes a dream seems more real than daylight, and you can't shake it out of your head. Only I've been having this dream on and off for months, and sometimes I'm not sure whether it's really happened, whether she really is someone I've met.

Her hair's the first thing you notice about her, loads of it, heavy auburn, the colour of unlikely sunsets, and smelling of patchouli. She's always walking away from me when I first see her, trailing wine velvet folds of an old long dress behind her.

I made the tea in the best teapot for a change. I could only find one mug, which meant the boys must have had lines of un-washed cups in their rooms, but I didn't fancy tea then, so it didn't matter. Somewhere upstairs the music started. Barry, I thought, but the music turned into rap, so it must have been Nelson. I couldn't get up the energy to shout, so I just kicked the hollow stair a couple of times. Barry, Nelson, I call them the boys but Barry must be two years older than me for a start off.

'Thanks, Wen,' said Ligsy when I handed him the mug. You could see his fingers were still cold, and he just held the mug for a while before he drank any of it. We watched the kids for a minute. Sheena's the image of Cayne – black straight hair, big blueish eyes, pointy chin, quick mind. Paula's more like me, tall, mousy. Paula's six now.

'I met Cayne outside the social. He said you'd got that spare room since Terry got put inside.'

I picked up the broken bit of Lego.

'He said to come and ask you,' he said.

'It's not like this place belongs to us, look, is it?' I said. 'We don't even rent it.'

'No, but fair do's Wen, everyone knows . . .'

'No, well they're mistaken aren't they, because we could be·

out any day, same as you. And I was keeping that room for Paula, now she's getting older she wants her own bedroom and Cayne bloody knows that.'

He was silent, looked down.

'We'll see,' I said. 'When did you get chucked out?'

'Bloody developers came round Thursday, posh, "I want you out by Saturday." Then this geezer turns up, the size of Frank Bruno, you don't argue, I'm telling you Wen, you don't argue. This bloke, I've seen him all over, like he works for these property developers. Last place I was in, it was him chucks us out.'

'Jesus,' I said. You could see they'd frightened him.

You had to sympathize with him, Ligsy's one of those people who always get themselves into trouble. Some people, you look at them and you know they're not lucky. He's got no – like cats survive, don't they, they somehow know how to, and some humans too, like me and Cayne, but Ligsy, he don't know how to look after himself. I saw him, sitting on my settee, looking at my kids like there's no problems, no tomorrows to worry about. The settee's a heap of shit, we got it out this skip on the Bayswater Road, but it says something about me and Cayne.

'Been sleeping out then?'

'Only one night, hostel the others. S'alright. I'm glad for a decent cup of tea though.' He grinned, shy.

'Is it time for the cartoons yet, Mummy?'

'No sweetheart, another hour and a half yet, you've only just had your dinner.' The afternoons get dark so quickly this time of the year.

'You want something to eat Ligs?'

'No, I'm fine, thanks,' he said. He was happy now. He took off his jacket and watched Paula and Sheena's game.

Typical, this. People know Cayne's soft hearted, so they ask him for help. And Cayne knows I can't say no straight to their faces. It's not like there's loads of room here though, there's five bedrooms, that's all. This place started off as a sort of co-operative, Cayne and me are the only ones left of the original lot who moved in, what six and a half years ago. It's a Victorian terraced house on the A40 and it was a real mess when we got here. Some old bloke had died and there was no relatives or something like that, you hear things, so we just moved in. The Council never bothered us for ages, then they said it was going to be sold then nothing happened. Cayne reckons they forgot about us, but I worry.

I was eight months pregnant with Paula when we moved in – my mum wouldn't let me stay at home when she found out I was having a baby, which is why me and Cayne came up here, and I'd got this mate Janice who said we could stay with her in her bedsit in Ladbroke Grove. Well we thought it would be easier in London. The bedsit was tiny though and when her landlord found out we were staying, he threw us all out.

And then we found this place. Cayne says it was a miracle, and that we got given this place for a reason, which is why he has always let people stay. He says we'll never get chucked out if we're kind with it. We've done all right, London's okay. It's not that much different from Southampton to be honest, more traffic, more people that's all.

Cayne was doing his plumbing training, day release and all that, he could have got qualified, but we came up here instead. He works on sites now and he's never been that much of a drinker so we get enough to live on. And he doesn't do drugs any more.

When I think of some of the dozy berks my mum wanted me to marry, I think I've been lucky. Cayne is quiet, rolls his cigs with the sort of look I see on Paula's face when she's trying to write her name, like there's nobody and nothing except that – that cig, that pencil – for a few moments. And he really likes everyone. I mean, he says he hates the government, but I bet you, if John Major came in for a chat and a cup of tea, Cayne would end up saying he was a good bloke.

Sometimes he annoys the hell out of me of course, like today, telling Ligsy he could stay when he knew we were going to let Paula have that room.

Ligsy got on the floor with the kids, elbows on the carpet, bum sticking up in the air. I could see his scrawny stomach as his jumper rid up.

'What you playing then?'

'Mrs Sanders is telling Sheena off because of her runny nose.'

'Haven't you got a hankie child?' said Sheena in her teacher voice.

'Then Cayne goes up the school and bashes her in,' said Paula, and the three of them started laughing.

'Bash bash bash,' said Sheena hitting the dolls together, laughing because the idea of Cayne hitting Mrs Sanders is so daft. I always have to go up the school on my own, he's that scared of her.

'Let's play lions now,' said Paula, organising, and they climbed on Ligsy's back while he went, 'Roar roar.'

Ligsy's not that far off being a kid himself, no more than eighteen. He hadn't brought any kit with him, so I went up-stairs to put a sheet on his bed.

The one thing you never get used to is the cold, and Ligsy's room was cold, no heating had been on in that room for weeks. Cayne's got this mate, and somehow he fixed us up to the elec-tricity so we don't have to pay. What I think is, some poor bas-tard up the road has to pay our bill, so I won't have the fires on in the bedrooms during the day, it's a rule, people can sit in the warm downstairs if they want to. Once I caught Nelson with the fire on in his room, and I gave him hell. I said, 'There's probably some old pensioner scrimping and saving just so's you can spoil yourself.' I've had a go at him loads of times, but his family are in Africa, so Cayne says whatever he does, he stays, he's got nowhere else.

The music had stopped. Out of the window I saw the buses and taxis and cars, endless and slow, and I could hear the hiss of their tyres on the wet road. It looked dismal out there, dark grey and soggy and cold. There's one tree in our front yard, leafless it was at the moment, but there was a bird on it anyway, at about the same height as where I was standing. Through the branches there were umbrellas bent forward so you couldn't see people's faces, just backs.

I put a clean sheet on the bed and some blankets, checked the light bulb was working and went downstairs.

The hallway was dark by now, I could hardly see the steps. I was almost at the bottom when the door knocker went again.

'Jesus, it's like Piccadilly Circus,' I said. 'Who is it?' I called to Paula, she could peek out of the front window.

Sheena started to try out, 'Piccadilly Circus Piccadilly Circus Piccadilly Circus.'

I stood in the doorway of the sitting room.

'It's a lady,' said Paula.

'Do we know her?'

'No,' said Paula and leaned her face on the glass to get a better look. 'Smart lady.'

'Get away from the window,' I said, but it was too late.

'She's seen me,' said Paula.

You have to open it if they've seen you, otherwise they send three people round next time.

'Hello,' she said. I couldn't see her properly, she was lit from behind by the street lamp, and glowed at the edges.

'I'm from –'

'Social Services,' we both said. You can always tell.

Social Services, what a joke, they're just Council, nosing,

they don't have a clue.

'Come in then.'

You never know what it is they've come about. Mrs Phillips was our normal one, a nasty woman in her forties, checking up on us, had we been claiming Social Security, where was Cayne if he wasn't working, what about family credit, were the children getting proper food, all that.

She followed me into the sitting room. Ligsy, Sheena and Paula were pretending to be cars.

'Brrmmmm,'

'Diccapilly Dirkers, Sickertilly Perters, Knickerfilly Burpers . . . hey, Knickerfilly Burpers!' Lots of hysterics.

'Oh good, Mr Robinson is here too,' said the social worker.

'No, he's just a friend.'

'Oh?' she said. It makes you sick, honestly, and I wasn't going to start explaining about Ligsy, it was none of her business.

I noticed a flash of her red hair as she turned round to take off her raincoat.

'Paula and Sheena not at school?' she said, to tell me she's done her homework, she knows my kids names.

'They've had the flu, why?' I said. 'The school been on to you, have they?'

I was beginning to wonder where I'd seen this woman's face, but she was looking down in her bag, getting out a file.

'Ligsy, go and make another pot of tea,' I said. He looked surprised.

'Oh,' he said, and swung off to the kitchen. He didn't know where anything was, and I figured he'd just sit there until she'd gone.

'Not for me,' said the woman, which is another thing they always say, in case your cups are dirty.

'Who are you then?'

'Oh I'm sorry, I should have said. Lisa Croft.' She stood up and put out her hand towards me, which I thought was a bit unnecessary, but I shook her hand.

I was able to get a proper look at her then, and I knew where I'd seen her before. She was the woman in my dream. Her hair was long, she can't have been any older than me, and her eyes were green and she was taller than me, and I'm tall for a woman. She wasn't wearing floaty clothes or anything, and she didn't smell of dope, but her hands, her mouth. She looked like she'd walked out of a castle.

We sat down at either ends of the settee. I looked at my old black jumper and tatty jeans and saw a shred of my dull hair hanging by my chin.

She said something which I didn't catch.

'Mrs Robinson?'

'I'm sorry,' I said, 'I was just thinking how lovely your hair is.'

She looked at me quickly, and then a funny thing happened. I saw her breathe in and her eyes go wet. And then I felt the rise in me too, and I tried to think of woolly hats, Lego, what's for tea. You have to push it down and talk and talk until you're safe again. I looked out of the window.

'Horrible isn't it,'

'Snow they said,' said Lisa Croft. 'Christ, London in the winter.'

'I'm wondering whether to get a proper fire going in here, but I'm not sure about the chimney.'

It's okay, it's okay, I said to myself, and then we could look at each other again. Sometimes I think there's a baby inside me who never shuts up.

'I only came to introduce myself. Mrs Phillips has retired and I've taken over from her. So, I thought – actually I'm not sure why you're on our books, but, anyway, if you ever want to talk, you know, or need any advice about benefits or any-thing . . .' She seemed to lose her track.

'You all right?' I said.

We both smiled, noticing it was me asking.

'Yes, I'm all right. Just moved into the area, it's all a bit new. It's a long way from Cheshire. Moving's always a wrench isn't it?'

I nodded. My father was in the navy. These six years is the longest I've lived anywhere.

'Anyway,' she continued, official, smiling again, 'if you ever need any help with the Council . . .'

'Are we going to be chucked out?' A sudden surprise of panic in me.

She looked surprised. 'No? Are you? Who told you that?'

'I suddenly wondered if that's why you came round.'

'No. Nobody has said anything. No, I'm sure you're okay. Well – ' She stood up to go.

After she'd gone I let Ligsy back into the sitting room. They put the cartoons on the television and I went into the kitchen to chop up the meat for the stew. I wished I could tell Cayne about her straight away, I knew he would be interested.

I always try to cook something hot for tea, shepherd's pie, or whatever. It takes ages, but I like the smell wafting round the house making you hungry hours before it's ready.

Cayne didn't get back in time for tea.

The kids and the boys ate theirs, Barry washed, Ligsy dried and Nelson made the pot of tea. Paula went up to the bedrooms to collect the dirty mugs, and then she made Nelson wash them since most of them had been hiding in his room. Then the boys had a teatowel fight, flicking each others legs and cursing each other. The girls loved it, but eventually I had to tell the boys to stop, Sheena and Paula were getting too excited to sleep, and I wanted them to go back to school the next day.

'Did Cayne say he was going to be late tonight?' I asked, because sometimes he's got something on, a mate to see, or a bit of night work, and he forgets to say anything. Barry shook his head, they're oldest mates, they were at school together. I never knew him then, we went to different schools.

'He never said anything to me,' said Ligsy. 'Maybe he went up the West End with Mark.'

Barry gave Ligsy a look.

'What?' said Ligsy, 'I was with Mark when I met Cayne outside the social this morning. They hadn't seen each other for ages, got chatting, and Cayne tells me to come over and see Wen. I don't know, what?'

The boys looked at me. Barry and I were remembering that the last time Mark came here he threw up all over the sitting room carpet.

I put the kids to bed, gave them hot water bottles, and then sat down in front of the telly for a while. When I went to bed I didn't take off any clothes, I put on another two jumpers and my bright blue thermal bedsocks which were a present from Nelson.

Mark Smith. Boring old Mark, red eyes, thin croaky voice, Parka the colour of dogshit. I had told Cayne I didn't like him.

I dreamt about her again. She was saying something and she wanted me to hear her but she had to keep on walking and I had to try to catch up with her. She moved quickly through the golden marble palace past pillars and windows. She was chanting something, and I ran to catch up, corridors and twists, so that I thought I would lose her. Then she stopped at a window and looked out at blue hills and distant rivers. She rubbed her fingers together and they made a rasping sound. And now I could hear her clearly:

'Lord now lettest thou thy servant depart in peace
lettest thou thy servant depart in peace

lettest thou thy servant depart . . .'

I woke when the front door opened, and got out of bed to listen.

'Shh.' Far too loud, Cayne.

'Orrf,' and someone tripped on the doormat, Mark. The sound of the sitting room door opening and whispers and then good-nights. Cayne's footsteps on the stairs. I got back into bed. I wouldn't say anything about Lisa Croft or Ligsy tonight, he was probably in no fit state.

Cayne took off his boots and got in next to me. I could smell the pub on him.

The ceiling was high and I could see car lights cross it from time to time. It was still raining. Cayne started breathing through his teeth. The noise got heavier and heavier until it was like the whole house was breathing at the same time. I pulled at his arm and he snorted and moved onto his side and was quiet.

David Rhymes

Along the N 340

While Jean-Paul drove, Sylvie read a paperback and smoked alternate blonde Gauloises and black Gitanes. And when she drove herself, she chewed chicle.

They set out with the sea behind them, reflected silver in the driving mirror, until it was replaced by an endless spool of grey highway, spilling out behind the car. They took turns at the wheel of the channel-green Fiat, cruising the N340 inland from Mojacar, south-west to Almeria, with their daughter, Felicite, asleep on the back seat. Jean-Paul drove one-handed with his free arm out of the window, his hand resting on the hot steel roof, but Sylvie gripped the wheel tightly and kept both eyes firmly on the road ahead.

When she occupied the passenger side, Sylvie loosened her seat-belt from time to time and screwed her body round in her seat to look at Felicite. The black-haired little girl was fast asleep each time she looked. One of her arms was continually falling off the cloth upholstery onto the floor, and with it, Bibi, her felt elephant. One time, Sylvie took a tissue out of her bag, stretched and wiped the child's mouth. Gently, so as not to wake her. And then she whisked a few hairs off her cheek and hooked them behind her ear.

Ninety kilometres short of their destination, the car began to overheat. They pulled over in a lay-by, agreeing without speaking to stop and give the engine time to cool. Jean-Paul opened the bonnet while Sylvie rummaged in the boot. She pulled her Walkman out of a beach-bag, put the pills in her ears and the compact in her pocket. She wandered away from the car, along the hot highway. Jean-Paul found half a litre of Evian Spring, unscrewed the radiator cap and poured it through a funnel.

Sylvie was listening to Miles Davis. She was dizzied by a glitter of cymbals, she was soothed a little by a string of soft, blue notes on the muted trumpet. Staring into hazy distance, she nearly stood on what was left of a cat. It lay there with its insides outside, rotting on the tarmac.

A pink tongue dangled out of its black mouth, flies buzzed in and out of its eyes, its gut was spread in coils across the tarmac. Both of its legs were tyre-pocked, its tail was glued to the road.

As she walked grimly back to the car she saw Jean-Paul slam the bonnet and wipe his hands on a rag. She could still taste sick in her mouth.

Half an hour later, they were ten kilometres short of the pueblo Vera. Sylvie was driving. She tried to overtake a fruit truck, but swerved out into the way of an oncoming Audi. The Audi's horn blared, its lights blazed. Sylvie was forced to fall back in line behind the truck. She was trembling. She was angry, but still she didn't speak. She focused her small black eyes on the spattered tail-gate in front and scowled. Jean-Paul was smirking behind his hand.

Two kilometres later, the truck turned off to the right, so everything might have been all right again. But Sylvie didn't speak to Jean-Paul, and Jean-Paul didn't say a word to Sylvie. Hour after hour of semi-desert landscape sweltered by, blurred and hazy under midsummer sky. They sped on in silence, a channel-green speck on a straight grey road, with the sun up high, like a golden zero.

Like a golden sovereign hung over the buff-brown land, an origin.

They passed village after village; chance after chance; each one leapt up at the side of the road, cast the temporary relief of shadow over the car, slid over the roof and shrank away. They saw strings of shuttered houses and deserted bars dissolve, grow distant as they rejoined the open plain. Each village had a solitary church and single road-side brothel; the church for sin, the brothel for confession; and Sylvie thought how much one was like the last.

They passed stubbly vineyards, orchards of oranges and peaches, vast polythene greenhouses and fields of rice as they drew closer to the sea.

And when they descended towards the silt plains of the Provincia de Almeria, tall trees lined the shade-spotted highway, mottling the car as it rumbled on. They cast stroboscopic flashes of light that gave Sylvie a headache.

The rhythm of her sighs suggested she was sick of driving. Jean-Paul took no notice. He pretended to read the map and then the guide-book.

*

It was two-thirty-two on the digital car clock when Sylvie geared down and eased the car onto a horseshoe of loose gravel outside a large hotel. Jean-Paul woke Felicite while Sylvie tied her hair back in the driving mirror. He lifted her out and kissed her awake. She woke up slowly and rubbed her eyes. She drank a little water, then wiped her face with a freshen-up square that Sylvie passed her. They were outside a large, whitewashed hotel on the outskirts of Almeria. Across the N340, the sea shimmered like a sheet of aluminium. It glittered over the iron-grey crash barriers, while fifty metres down, it lapped against the foot of sheer cliffs. At Sylvie's height it was metallic; at beach level, a kind of crystal cobalt.

Traffic flew in both directions along the raised highway.

The family made their way into a restaurant attached to the hotel. They sat down at a low table and waited. When at last someone came over to deal with them, Sylvie ordered clams, prawns, salad and fizzy water.

Jean-Paul lit up a cigarette and squashed the packet with one hand.

Sylvie read the menu again.

Felicite looked out of the window at the sea.

When the food came, the family ate in silence, more bread than anything.

Back in the car, Jean-Paul took his seat behind the wheel and Sylvie thumbed through the Michelin guide, looking for a page she'd folded down. There was a map, with details of a campsite they'd chosen back at home. It was located at the western edge of Almeria, about a kilometre short of Aguadulce. The site was called Las Gaviotas, which Jean-Paul said meant seagulls.

He looked over Sylvie's shoulder while she read, and Felicite pressed her cheeks between the two front seats. All three pored over the map. Sylvie pointed and Jean-Paul nodded once quickly.

Sylvie watched the sea as they sped along the last stretch of the N340. She saw boats moored or beached in bays that were visible from the highway. Felicite pointed at the horizon, where a boat was gliding out on the air.

It was half past four.

Sylvie saw the sign. She tapped Jean-Paul's arm and pointed. Felicite cheered and put on her sunglasses. She looked like a six year old Jackie Onassis.

Las Gaviotas gave a welcome of white flagpoles, each with a European flag flying at full mast, making a windswept line of primary colour that fringed the sloping approach road. Sylvie helped Felicite to recognise and count them off.

Italy, France, Germany, Sweden . . .

Jean-Paul left the engine running and got out of the car. He went into a wooden shack that served as a reception.

When he came back, Felicite was puzzling over a blue flag with a ring of yellow stars. Sylvie was giving her clues. Jean-Paul dipped his head through her window and asked her to follow him down to their emplacement in the car. Sylvie gave him a queer look.

A look that said, 'And if I don't?'

Jean-Paul struck the roof of the car and cursed under his breath.

'What's the matter with daddy?' said Felicite as Sylvie swapped seats.

'Oh, nothing. Nothing Feli. He's just a little bit tired. It's very tiring you know, driving. Never mind. We're here now. Isn't it lovely?'

Sylvie put the car in gear and inched down the slope behind Jean-Paul. He was talking to a man in ragged black overalls who was pointing and waving his hand.

She saw lines of tents pitched under plane trees at either side of the lane, bright summery canvases, cool and in ample shade. At the foot of the hill, she saw a viaduct. The grey-blue sea glittered under its arches. Children were running about in the shade.

For a moment, she wanted to take her foot off the brake and roll down the hill, crushing Jean-Paul as she went.

She would just keep on driving, over Jean-Paul, under the arches, across the small pebbled beach and into the sea. She would drive straight into the sea and just keep on going until a swirl of blue and silver salt water had swallowed up the car.

But she didn't. She held the steering wheel lightly in her hands. She inched down the slope behind Jean-Paul and pulled up at an empty emplacement.

'Why is daddy angry?' said Felicite.

'Why don't you ask daddy?' said Sylvie, and got out of the car.

*

She stood ankle deep in water and felt the slick of waves draw shale and scuzz against her ankles. She felt the cool caress of water and its subtle relaxation of the ground beneath her feet.

She felt as if she were submerged, reaching out for something ill-defined and shapeless, suspended in the murk and changing.

It was so like drowning she was scared.

Swaddled like a baby, cocooned, in chrysalis, shielded from the memory of that, of this, of everything, she stirred the shale with her toe and saw, through the spangles, a bright refraction of herself reflected back and angled. She waded up to her waist and brushed the surface with her outstretched fingers.

She splashed silver droplets on her body, soaked her arms and shoulders, stretched and swallow-dived. A single deep stroke and the waters of the ocean wrapped around her.

She was engulfed in clear green, flowing free of herself and swimming from the solid substance of the earth into the soft and pliant sea.

She rolled over onto her back and heard the salt sea crackle as she scanned the shore.

A milky mist had dropped down over the road, and the cliffs were vague behind. Below the road, the long shadows of acacia trees stretched out like forks of lightning on the path. There was the faintest hint of a storm in the sky.

Now it was cool and nearly dark; now the fierce hunger in the heat had subsided; under the damp screen of early evening, now the ocean was huge and flat and green. Now, thought Sylvie, now.

Felicite came under the arch of the viaduct, down to the edge of the beach and waved. Sylvie waved back. She swam smoothly to the shore, stumbled out of the water and dripped up the beach to her shoes. She put them on, slung a towel around her back and shivered. She walked slowly up the beach to the path. She felt better.

'Daddy's done the tent,' said Felicite.

'Has he?' said Sylvie.

Felicite nodded. 'He's going to fill in the register too.'

'Oh, good.'

'And he says he isn't angry.'

'That's good because it's silly to be angry. Here.'

Sylvie gave Felicite a razor shell. The creature had long since gone and the sea had worn it smooth. Felicite stared at it. She slid it gently into her pocket.

'Are you ever angry mummy?' she said.

Sylvie thought for a moment. 'Sometimes,' she said, and sighed. Felicite listened to her carefully.

'Sometimes things can happen to make a person angry. It's not always that the person wants to be angry, it's just that sometimes things happen that confuse the person and they lose control. It's perfectly natural.'

Felicite thought for a moment.

'Are you angry now mummy?' she said quietly.

Sylvie clapped her hands brightly and laughed.

'Feli! How could anyone be angry here?'

*

'Tonight and tomorrow night in the city. Fiesta. Very fine Fiesta. *Preciosa!*' The boy took Sylvie's money and gave her change. One or two drops of condensation ran off the bottles onto her skirt as she read the labels.

'You should go,' he said. 'Your little girl would love it.'

Sylvie smiled and put the bottles in her bag. 'Tonight?'

'Tonight. Eight o'clock.'

She nodded. 'Eight o'clock.'

'Might see you there then,' said the Spanish boy.

'Yes,' said Sylvie. 'Maybe.'

He locked his till and followed them outside. Felicite glanced back at him and smiled.

'*Hola nina*', he said. '*Que tal?*'

Sylvie took her hand.

'That's Spanish,' she said in French.

Felicite nodded.

'Does daddy know there's a fiesta?' she said in French.

'I don't know,' said Sylvie. She shrugged and opened her cigarettes.

'Fiesta . . .' said Felicite, drawing a long breath.

*

When they got back, Jean-Paul was sitting on the wall behind the tent.

'I think we should go for something to eat soon,' he said. Sylvie rubbed a towel through her hair.

'OK,' she said. 'If you drive.'

'OK I'll drive. If you cheer up. It can't be that bad.'

Sylvie threw back her head. 'It's worse,' she said.

She saw Jean-Paul grind a cigarette nub under his foot.

'Nice swim?' he said after a pause.

'So so,' said Sylvie. She threw her towel onto the roof of the car.

Felicite listened. She nestled against Jean-Paul's legs as he made another cigarette. He wafted one or two hairs out of her eyes and she wrinkled up her nose. Sylvie looked at them sideways through a web of hair.

'Mummy,' said Felicite, detaching herself. 'Please can we go?'

Sylvie smiled. 'Of course we can Feli. We can go to the shop for a snack first if you like. How about an ice cream? Are you hungry?'

Felicite made a hungry noise and rubbed her tummy. Sylvie laughed and went on combing her hair. It was long and black and shone like molasses.

Kirkham Jackson

Sunday to Saturday

Sunday
Not sure how best to approach this journal/diary – whether to just write down the day's events or to include some of the ideas I've been having. I suppose I know the answer to that question before I've finished putting it down. What I need right now is some order to all the things that have been on my mind. Get them down on paper and not forever swimming round my brain. Too many things are going on for me to hope they'll just take care of themselves. Decisions are being made.

But something else is happening, which I seem to have no control over. For a start there are too many coincidences – too many for them all to be just coincidence. For example at exactly 2.05 am every night I wake up. I'll only have been asleep for a couple of hours but suddenly I'm sitting bolt upright in bed, staring at the clock which always says 2.05. Is that time significant? Is that the time of day I'm going to die, perhaps – pre-destined, and somehow I've caught a glimpse of it? There are days when I have no idea what's going on, when I'm completely lost.

My mum has been in my dreams a good deal lately. Last night I dreamt we were lying in her bed together like we used to do on Sunday mornings. I had the body of a six year old but my thoughts were grown-up. I can't remember what we said now, perhaps we didn't say anything, but I know it felt good being there. It's funny, but as I get older, I feel more like a sister to her than a daughter. Some of the things she said and did when I was young and her reasons for doing them seem clearer to me now. She was just trying to make a bit of room for herself. I'm beginning to understand that.

It's now two months since I gave up meat and men, though I still eat tuna. If slimy Malcolm dares to nose his Peugeot up my drive again I'll smash it with my spade. I'll dent his precious bodywork in so many places and with such vigour they'll have to call the fire brigade to get him out. That'll set his car alarm off.

Some men seem to just trundle through their lives bouncing blindly from one woman to the next; seem to wilfully ignore the experience and self-knowledge that's staring them right in the face. They are oblivious to change. They grow fat, go bald but persist with the pretence that they're still a teenager. No-one says to them, 'God, just look at you. What a bloody mess.' Eg: Malcolm.

It was my birthday the day before yesterday. I made an aubergine bake and a green salad, drank a bottle and a half of Sainsbury's Bordeaux and got a little morose. I did some sums. I tried to work out, over the twenty five years that my body's been monthly going to war with itself, exactly how many paracetamols I must have shovelled into my mouth, how many hot water bottles I've held to my stomach. Mountains of them, I imagine. Yet no matter how hard I clutch a cushion to me, there is still a pain, an emptiness.

Monday
This morning did all the shopping. Called at the supermarket and stocked up with the usual stuff plus some babyfood/milk and disposable nappies. Then, took a deep breath and marched into Mothercare. Bought some feeding bottles, two blankets (one pink, one blue) and a little striped babysuit. The shop assistant who served me was very helpful, which I much appreciated. Stopped in at the toy shop I've always liked the look of and bought . . . a telephone with a big smile on its face, a cuddly toy (tiger) and some colouring books and crayons. I

had no idea toys were so expensive. Asked the woman behind the counter (who seemed so worldly and amiable) if she thought it true that women who hadn't actually given birth could still breast-feed. I'd heard something about it on the radio. She got quite flustered and stared at me like I was completely bonkers, so I just paid for the things and got out of there as quick as I could.

I was getting quite nervous about everything but gave myself a good talking to, calmed down and had a nice vegetarian lasagne for lunch while reading a book. As I was doing the washing-up a most peculiar thing happened. I sneezed (presumably from the smell of the soap) and a shower of pink blossom fell from the tree out in the garden, just a few yards from my face. It was as if the force of my sneeze had dislodged them. Now my common sense tells me there is no possibility of the two things being connected. A gust of wind must have simultaneously blown through the garden. I *know* that. But it felt, somehow, as if I'd been set up. Like someone was having a joke at my expense.

Couldn't keep still for the rest of the afternoon. In the end I went for a walk then did any housework I hadn't already done. The house is *spotless*.

Tonight watched a bit of TV and left a note for the milkman ordering an extra pint, which left me quite giddy. Managed to relax (had a stiff drink) and read a book in bed.

Just now, my mind drifted back to some of the toys I'd seen in the shop this morning. There was one in particular which started off as a car, but when you opened the doors it began unfolding into something quite different. Its chassis split in two and an ugly monster-head emerged from under the bonnet. Before you knew it, it had transformed itself into a nasty sort of space-creature. I just know I'm going to dream about it tonight.

Tuesday

She's beautiful. She lies beside me on my bed as I write, with pillows twice her size all around her to stop her rolling off. She breathes her small baby-breaths, tucked-up in sleep.

I don't know her real name, so I call her Rachel – no idea why. She must be between one and one and a half and she can toddle. In fact she very nearly toddled right off the top of the stairs this evening. I nearly died of fright. How are you supposed to keep an eye on them all the time? How do you bring up a child without living in a constant state of anxiety? All day she's wandered around the house, picking things up, examining them and, more often than not, putting them in her mouth. I hadn't realised how many objects lay within a child's grasp around my house that were either too valuable to me or too dangerous for her to play with. It's made me look at my surroundings in quite a new light.

When she first arrived she cried and cried – who'd have imagined such terrifying sounds could be made by such little lungs? Her face was all red and contorted. But I got the tiger out and gave her a biscuit and she gradually calmed herself down, thank God. If she'd cried much longer I'm sure I'd have gone quite mad.

With a baby around the place, something as simple as preparing a meal becomes ten times more difficult. Half one's attention is forever following the baby; wondering where she is, what she's up to. If she was making some noise it wasn't so bad, but a sudden hush would convince me she was choking on something or lying unconscious. After a few hours I no longer felt like a complete human being. Part of my mind was traipsing after Rachel. I felt dissipated.

She'd been here most of the day before I realised I hadn't checked to see if she needed changing. She did. Took me almost an hour to do it. In the end she was so dirty I ran a bath and the two of us climbed in.

Today has been the happiest (and longest) day of my life. We've done a thousand things and have been getting along famously. By early evening we were both washed out. Her eyes were closing against her will and she kept rubbing her ears as if they itched, but she adamantly refused to drop off. I had her in my arms and was walking her up and down, up and down, talking to her in whispers. Then, quite out of the blue, she began screaming. I thought something terrible had happened, like something inside her had broken. She pulled that frightful face and huge tears began tumbling down her cheeks. I thought she'd never stop. Christ, what a racket! She kicked and pushed herself out of my arms but when I put her down she screamed even more. So I just kept walking her up and down, rocking her in my arms. Eventually, out of sheer desperation, I started singing to her the first thing that came into my head, which was that old Andy Williams song . . . 'Wise men say only fools rush in, but I can't help falling in love with you.' God knows where that came from. I must have sung those two lines over and over a hundred times – I couldn't remember any more of it. After a while, she began to quieten down. Then, to my amazement, she dozed off, her little head against my shoulder. It was like a miracle.

I was convinced the slightest jar would wake her up again so I kept on singing under my breath, rocking her gently to and fro. I could feel the vibration of my voice in her little body and saw on the wall a shadow cast by the lamp of me with her in my arms. I moved over to the mirror, slowly, afraid she'd wake up and start screaming again. She was like a little bomb, ready to go off. I inched my way over until, at last, there she was. Her tiny eyes closed, nuzzling against me. Me with a baby in my arms. Me crying.

I know that somewhere her mummy and daddy must be thinking about her, wondering where she is. I dearly wish there were some way I could let them know that she's fine, that I'm taking care of her.

Wednesday

She stirred a couple of times in the night, but the bottle of milk I'd made up last night seemed to do the trick. We were both awake by 7.30, refreshed and ready to face a new day. I dressed her in her new outfit and she seemed very pleased with it. We were getting along splendidly, making toast and pottering about the kitchen when I made the mistake of flicking on the TV. I thought there might be a cartoon or something light-hearted for us to watch, but it was the usual global round-up of suffering and disaster. Then the local news came on and there was a whole piece about little Rachel going missing. They showed the supermarket where the pram was parked and some stupid little man from the store saying how his company couldn't be held responsible and how parents should be more careful where they leave their babies. Little runt! Who the hell is he to preach to parents? I could tell by his attitude that he'd no children of his own. No self-respecting woman would go near him. The reporter said the police were asking for witnesses. Witnesses! They make it sound like a murder. I'm worried now that the whole thing could get blown out of all proportion. She can't go back yet – we're just beginning to get to know each other.

Actually, perhaps the man from the supermarket had a point. Maybe mums and dads should be more careful with their babies. In some ways, it was a good job I came along.

Am beginning to wish I'd left a note or message of some sort, explaining what I was doing. Saying not to worry. Maybe I should ring the police and tell them it's all right? Perhaps they'd be able to trace the call? Besides, they wouldn't understand.

Switched off the set and just knew that the morning was

spoilt. I'd had all manner of exciting things planned but that really took the shine off them.

About 10 o'clock, went for a walk round the park. Felt very conspicuous. Seemed like people were looking at Rachel's little face to see if it matched the one on the news. Kept ourselves very much to ourselves.

We fed the ducks on the pond but both got nervous when they came a bit too close and tried to snatch the bread from our hands. One of them in particular kept looking at Rachel, the way ducks do. He looked as if he was about to gobble her up. I felt like saying, 'Hey you! Just you stop that! For your information, I have recently given up meat of all kinds. I don't eat your little friends, so why don't you just show some respect?' Its beady little duck-eyes kept staring at her, as if it was thinking, 'Yeah, that's the one – that's the baby that was on the news this morning.'

In the end I had to shoo them away and we went straight home to lunch. That's the last time those mangy old birds get any bread from me. They can starve to death as far as I'm concerned.

I knew it was a mistake to switch on the lunchtime news but I couldn't help it, I was curious. I started thinking maybe it wasn't Rachel they were talking about this morning. Maybe another baby had gone missing and I was getting confused. Or maybe it would all have blown over. But ten minutes after I'd switched on there was a special little piece about it. It was terribly upsetting. There was a telephone number people could ring with information. And on top of all this, Rachel's mummy and daddy were interviewed in their front room, holding a photograph of her. They were crying and begging for the person who took her to please bring her back. They kept calling her Samantha, not Rachel. And I couldn't help but notice how poorly off they were. Their furniture looked as though it had come from the Salvation Army – all formica and pot horses. It occurred to me that, financially, I'm actually in a far better position to bring up a child than they are.

Strange seeing a grown man cry on television – quite disturbing. And they were neither of them anything like what I'd imagined. The daddy was bald. Imagine that, a bald daddy.

Turned the TV off in disgust. Rachel had been pretending not to watch but she knew very well what was going on.

Our whole day was in ruins and all my big plans felt like they were collapsing around my ears. I was so annoyed I could barely speak.

Later on, I was checking the drive to make sure no-one was hanging around and when I went back into the living room I caught Rachel on the telephone. She put the receiver down quick as a flash and busied herself with something else. I said to her, very calmly, 'Who were you ringing just now, Rachel? Who were you calling?' Not a word. She simply glared at the carpet, like she didn't have a clue what I was talking about, but I just knew she'd been calling that number off the TV. You'd think little babies would have difficulty remembering long numbers. Maybe she wrote it down somewhere when I wasn't looking. Anyway, I was furious and barely managed to keep a grip. I snatched the phone from her and she burst into guilty tears. The telephone still wore its inane grin and I swear I could have happily thrown it on the fire. But quite calmly, I took the scissors, cut through the wires and put it on the highest shelf I could find. Did the same to all the other phones in the house.

All this time little Rachel bawled her head off. I had to pick her up and comfort her, if only to get her to be quiet. After a few minutes she seemed suitably repentant – as if accepting that she'd perhaps acted a little rashly and put lots of potential fun in jeopardy. We talked it through and having done so, both felt a good deal better for it.

Spent a glorious couple of hours with the colouring books

and at one point Rachel took the initiative and crayoned onto the wall. Things quickly got out of hand, wonderfully so, until, by the time we'd come to our senses, we'd crayoned everything within crayoning distance – the television, the furniture, our clothes and faces.

Ate giggling like schoolgirls, had another nice long bath and played some Schubert to calm us down. When she's grown up, little Rachel will be fond of classical music, unlike all her contemporaries. It will set her apart. Like me, her favourite composers will be Schubert and Mahler. When she hears them she'll think of these first happy days. Perhaps I'll encourage her to learn an instrument. The violin. Or the cello. Strange how a familiar piece of music becomes so loaded with memory, so that only a few bars of it is enough to tug at the emotions and send them unravelling all over the place. The Schubert got me quite upset and had to have a couple of drinks to put myself straight. Poor Rachel seemed quite mystified by it all.

Managed to get her off to sleep about an hour ago and she lies next to me, dreaming her little dreams, with her tiny hands holding onto the bedclothes.

I'm in no state to make decisions, though they demand to be made. I feel myself being pulled in a dozen different directions at once; my head threatens to overflow with thoughts. All evening I'd kept coming back to Rachel's parents weeping on TV and Rachel trying to get word to them on the telephone. What she might have said to the police if I'd not interrupted her and what she might have had time to say while I was out. It dawned on me while I was doing the washing-up what information she would have given them – the thing that sets my house apart, its one identifying feature. The cherry tree. How many flowering cherry blossoms could there be in this town? Hardly any number at all. It seemed so obvious I could have kicked myself for not thinking of it before. That's what she'd have told them. I can hear her little voice saying, 'I am being kept at a house with a big garden. There is a pink tree.'

I imagine policemen clambering aboard helicopters – flying low over the houses, on the look out for cherry blossom. At least it's still dark. It's late but I still have some thinking to do.

Thursday

No sky today. There is no sky. This is not a new day, I know it. It's old, second-hand. A day from last year, regurgitated. A big trick.

This morning, before the sun could pretend to be in the sky, I took Rachel round to the police station, lifted her little body up onto the big wooden counter and walked out before anybody could attend to me, our life together terminated. She had a note pinned to her new striped jumpsuit explaining everything.

Chopped down my beloved cherry blossom and stuffed all the bits into plastic bags. Felt like a murderer. No-one will ever know how it broke my heart to have to do that. When I'd done, all that remained was a stump surrounded by a thousand tell-tale petals, like a bird after a cat has finished with it.

I will avoid the television and its inevitable footage of the reunion, the tears of joy. We made a deal, Rachel and I. She would return to her strange mummy and daddy and neither of us would say anything more to anyone of our little adventure. Our secret. Perhaps she'll visit me when she's older.

The bin men came chugging up the drive just now, all beer-guts, beards and bottoms. One of them knocked on the door and said they couldn't possibly take all the bits of tree, how it was more than they were supposed to accept from any one household. But he wore a smirk on his face that quite blatantly suggested a few pounds would make all the difference. I pro-duced a five pound note and he went off looking pleased as

Punch. I watched from the window as they collected the bags and was horrified to see, bound to the radiator of their wagon, a bedraggled teddy bear and a dolly with both arms missing, all grimy and sodden and sad. They looked like little hostages, being paraded through the city streets. Who could possibly derive any pleasure from such brutality? And who but men would think of doing such a thing?

I will try and get to sleep. I have so much to sort out that my brain is completely locked. There is too much. It will have to wait until later. I will start later. Perhaps when I wake, a small gap might have appeared and I can start on it, like a Chinese puzzle.

I try and sleep but every time I close my eyes I have the sound of Rachel crying in my ears. It is not my imaginination. They are echoes, real echoes – the deposits of her short stay here, ringing in my head.

Simon Christmas

Rubric for a Pretended Family

from *Rubric for a Pretended Family*

As soon as she walked into the room, with its familiar faint scent of age and urine, Joan could discern death among the fragrances.

She put down the cup of tea she was carrying on the bedside table and tried to shake the still warm body awake, failing, as most people, to trust her animal senses; but she succeeded merely in shaking more of the odour into the atmosphere. She checked for a pulse. And only when she could not feel the persistent rhythm in the wrist did she believe what she knew anyway. Odd, she thought, that this evidence should convince her when she usually could not find her own. Rather foolishly she checked it now, and for once there it was, pumping its little heart out and quite oblivious to whether she might be listening or not. For a brief moment she almost resented its being there under her skin, like a parasite, no more a part of her than if it were a tap dripping in another room.

And then she shook all that nonsense from her head and said 'No,' which she found a comforting word. A word, moreover, which kept things in proportion. Stay calm, begin at the beginning, carry on until you come to the end. She would begin by ringing Nick.

It wasn't until the phone had rung out at the other end a few times that she realised she was being stupid and that Nick would already be in at work, but before she could put the receiver down the ringing stopped abruptly and Nick's voice sleepily announced his telephone number.

'Oh,' she said, 'you are there. I was just about to try you at work.'

'Hi Mom,' said Nick. He was naked, having been roused from his bed by the phone, and the room was freezing cold, and as he spoke he picked up a sweat-shirt that lay nearby and tried to negotiate it over his head without taking in the receiver. 'I'm not in this morning.'

'No. Did I wake you? I'm sorry.'

'No problem.'

There was the tiniest of pauses, just long enough for Nick to wonder if it was he who had phoned his mother rather than vice versa.

'I'm afraid I've got bad news, dear,' said Joan. 'Your grandad passed away in the night.' And she thought of her boy having to hear this all on his own in that awful place. It would upset him more than anyone.

By now Nick was awake enough to have worked out why the sweat-shirt which he was struggling to put on did not fit — which was because it did not belong to him, it belonged to the body which belonged to the arm which he had had to remove from his chest before running shivering to the phone. The body, moreover, was now sitting up, the duvet gripped about its shoulders, laughing at the sight of Nick naked but for its own red sweat-shirt over his head and half of one arm, oblivious to the news Nick had just received.

Nick glared at it and said in a loud voice — with no particular thoughts about intonation — 'Dead.'

The body shut up.

'Yes,' said Joan, who foolishly thought it was she to whom her son was talking. 'It was all very peaceful. In his sleep.'

Only now did Nick appreciate the word he had spoken. 'Hold on,' he said. 'I'm sorry, can you start again.'

'It was in his sleep, I said. So there was no pain.'

'No,' said Nick, waving a hand which Joan could not of course see. 'Before that.'

Joan was confused. 'Before?'

Nick could hardly say 'Before I picked up the phone,' and even that would not have been early enough.

'No,' he said, 'I mean . . . I'm sorry, I was asleep, I'm confused a bit.'

Joan looked at the clock as if it might tell her what to do, but said nothing. It was a grandfather clock, but she did not notice this rather obvious little irony.

'You're saying . . .' began Nick, but that was silly. 'When did this happen?' So was that really. 'I mean when did you find out?'

'Just this minute. Literally just now. I came straight to ring you. I've not even called the doctor or anything yet.' And then, just in case Nick might feel there was still some doubt until the doctor came, she added: 'But I've already checked for a pulse.'

'And there was none?'

'No. There wasn't. But I suppose I might have missed it.'

'Mother, surely it's obvious if somebody is dead.'

'Oh. Yes of course.'

Nick looked across at the body, which was looking sympathetic all over its fat face. He remembered that it belonged to someone called Duncan, and that he had thought a great deal of it and its owner the night before. But, what was it, the cold light of day? Something like that. It caught him out every time.

Joan, who had been trying vainly to see her son over the hundred and fifty miles of wire between them, interrupted his silence: 'Look, dear, shall I ring back?'

'No,' said Nick, turning away to face a tattered old print of Rousseau's *La Guerre*, the only detail of his damp, cramped flat which still appealed to him. 'No, it's OK, I just . . . What happens now? Is there anything I need to do?'

'There will have to be a funeral.'

'Yes, of course. Yes. OK, well, when will that be?'

'I don't know. I can let you know though. Early next week

I suppose. He wanted to be cremated. I think that's quicker. To organise I mean.'

'OK, well I'll sort it out with work and come home this evening.'

'There's no need to rush back, dear. I don't want you to get into trouble or anything. I haven't rung Chris yet but I can't see him coming until the last moment possible. You're not expected . . .'

'I know I'm not.'

'Well, if you want to come now you're very welcome of course.'

'I expect I can help out?'

'Oh, everything's under control.'

'Well look, I'll see you tonight then.'

'If you like then.'

'I don't know what time. I'll give you a ring before I leave. OK?'

'There's no need to worry.'

'I'll speak to you later then. Bye.'

'Goodbye love.'

She sat a moment in her telephone chair after putting the phone down. Perhaps it was as well that Nick was coming home. He was sure to be upset, and maybe she could lessen his grief a little. Although she sometimes felt, from the distance to which her love for him had banished her, that sadness had become a way of life for him, and that the days of her helping were past. But no. She shook herself. She needed to ring Chris as well, or rather, since Chris would be at work, Sue; and then she needed to call the doctor – or should she do that first? – and the undertaker, and then her sisters and the rest of the family would have to be told. Perhaps she would have a cup of tea first though. And then she remembered that she had never brought her father's teacup down, and went to get it, wondering as she went up whether she oughtn't call the doctor while waiting for the kettle to boil.

'You haven't touched your tea then,' she said to her father when she found the teacup still full, then, after a moment: 'No. Of course.'

Nick's first reaction once he had put down the receiver was to pull the hateful sweat-shirt right off. As he did so there was a ripping sound.

'Oh,' he said, examining the hole in the armpit, 'sorry.'

The body, or rather Duncan, waved his arm dismissively. 'Oh don't mind that,' he said, but he might just as well have said 'My clothing is as nothing next to whatever loved one you may have lost.'

'I'll get you a new one,' said Nick, knowing very well he would be doing no such thing. He unhooked his dressing gown from the door and put that on instead, although he was so frozen by now that clothes seemed irrelevant.

'Would you like me to go?' asked Duncan, thoughtfully.

'No, no, not at all.'

Duncan nodded in a way that was meant to be an assurance of continued sympathy, but since Nick wasn't actually looking at him he let the gesture lapse into a concerned rocking motion. 'Was it someone very close to you?'

But Nick was busy rooting through one of the draws of his desk for a train timetable to Shrewsbury, and had just come across a leaflet from a promotion of fresh cream in Sainsbury's which made him smile, because he had told the sweet little man who had been handing them out that he was only interested if the little man put his phone number on it, and they had ended up going for a bizarre dirty weekend in the Isle of Wight at the house of the little man's estranged wife, who brought them tea in bed in the morning and read to them from Leviticus while they were drinking it. Joshua his name had been.

'Pardon,' he said, looking up.

'Was it someone very close to you?'

'Oh. My grandfather? Yes, we were very close. I suppose he was a sort of father to me. My father left when I was very small so . . .' It occurred to him that really it was his mother, if anyone, who would be most upset, for she had so little else.

Duncan's rocking had picked up speed for another nod. 'It will take a while to sink in. I know, my great aunt died two months back – of course it's nothing like the same thing – but still, I was very fond of her. And it takes a while to get used to the idea.'

'Yes,' said Nick, none too interested in Duncan and his great aunt, and wishing both would go. 'Do you want some coffee?' And he escaped to the kitchen.

But it was as he got two cups down from the cupboard that it suddenly became very important that it was two – that there was a second cup to be made – so important indeed that he made neither, but went straight back to the bedroom, only to find himself with no idea what it was that he was to say when he got there. He stood in silence, as if trying to find the right words for some great declaration. Which was all wrong.

'Are you OK?' asked Duncan.

'Yeah,' said Nick, chewing his fingernail. 'Yes, I'm fine. I just . . . Well, I just thought, it's odd really, that's all. I mean, I haven't seen him since last Christmas, so, I haven't seen him in ages. And it's just odd, you know.'

Duncan, sitting with the duvet wrapped around him like a shawl, moved himself to lean back against the wall, and the thought of the warmth of the newly created space and of well fleshed Duncan drew Nick into both. He sat on the bed's edge, so that Duncan might enfold him in bedspread wings and hold him there, and for a while they sat like that in silence as Nick tried to reconstruct a face for his loss. But he kept losing things – an eye, a nose, a smile – in the intrusive and inanimate clutter of the hateful flat.

Duncan, although his left leg was beginning to get pins and needles, didn't like to say anything.

'When I was little . . .' thought Nick aloud, forgetting to say any more, or really think it, come to that.

'Yes?' said Duncan, taking the opportunity to move his leg as well. But even such a small change broke the stasis that had briefly held Nick, who felt as if propelled forwards by the force of the movement.

'Oh,' he said dismissively, getting to his feet and re-belting his dressing gown. 'I was just thinking about the stories he used to tell me. You know, when I was a kid.' And he smiled wryly to himself – at the stories, the games they had inspired, the ends to which they and he had come, the distance in between.

'I'm going to go into Town,' he said, deciding it didn't matter what he did as long as he got out of his flat quickly. He thought of Trafalgar Square, so open, he would go there. And he would get to everything else later: packing, finding that timetable, ringing into work, where he should have been, whatever he'd told his mother, and now he'd promised to ring her as well of course, but all this was so much more clutter, so he'd just go out.

He had first fallen in love with Trafalgar Square when he had been able to buy it for £240 and build houses on it. He had liked it then because there was a Chance card that said 'Advance to Trafalgar Square,' and this had always seemed a very grand notion, far grander than advancing to Pall Mall or Mayfair, which were mere streets. Not Squares, Trafalgar Square, a great intersection, a central point which the traffic converged upon, whisked around and was spun out in new directions. That was what thrilled him, the rumble and roar of the buses and taxis and cars sucked through the square in the same way that computer simulations of Voyager had shown the space probe spinning past the masses of Jupiter or Saturn and catapulted by the fine play of forces out to some yet farther planet. Or was that it, that he sat at the centre of gravity, there to be taken seriously, and watched by the world that spun about Nelson's Column – no, better, about himself, all the activity and noise centred upon him? Trafalgar Square. Advance to Trafalgar Square. Advance to Go, though Nick didn't know where that actually was.

Duncan stood waiting while he mortice-locked the door, then preceded him down the spiral of steps sprung to the walls of the too spacious stairwell. Duncan's curls, that had the night before been combed each into place, bobbed at the level of Nick's waist, and bore his gaze round and round and always down. It was he who had broken their gelled arrangement with tender and then grasping hands: and so, another image shattered as soon as reached for.

Out on the street, over the bricks and greys and brown stained fences, patches of colour were scattered like sweet wrappers in a gutter. The neon clothes of children, bright primary clothes on signs mapping the estates (You are Here, but things are not as painted), red and blue of traffic signs, blue watered into grey on the balconies of a concrete hulk facing, blue lost in grey across the humped sky. And sweet wrappers too.

Nick's grandfather, lover of flowers, had one day in summer spied a bloom on his Rosa Floribunda Dorothy Wheatcroft from his seat by the window. A small orange blossom amongst the showier clusters of red. He had surprised Nick's mother when he came stumbling through the kitchen on his way out: it wasn't so warm, he would need a coat on anyway. She had been curious, concerned even, he seemed short of breath, as if excited, and after watching his progress across the lawn a while she had thrown on a cardigan and followed. 'There,' he said crossly when she reached him by the rose bush. 'It's just a bit of paper.' A Toffee Crisp wrapper.

Perhaps he had thought that there in his garden bees had cross-pollinated and genes mutated, and a new species had been born. That was what they had assumed, Nick and his mother, when she told the story on the phone, and they laughed about it.

'What line is it here?' asked Duncan, prompted by a train passing above them to their right.

'Docklands. Or East London.'

Duncan thought, or rather, Duncan fell silent, and pulled a thoughtful face, and Nick surmised that he thought, and looked away. A boy, dressed entirely in green, was watching him over a fruit juice carton from a doorway across the street, and only slurped when Nick smiled. All this, thought Nick, all this construction of melancholy, sadness rotting at the concrete, all this could be cleared away, with determination. All this could be better.

'If I get the East London line up to Whitechapel then and change there,' mused Duncan.

'Ah,' said Nick, giving the straw-chewing child a last stern glance. 'You're just up there then,' – pointing, there being Shadwell Station, incongruously cheerful in its modern, curvaceously protuberant and red framed glass fashion. 'I go up here,' – nodding, here being Shadwell II, son of Shadwell, a flight of steps up to the lofty Light Railway. Duncan frowned and rubbed the fold of his nose where a spot was growing.

'Or I could get the Docklands to Tower Gateway and change there. To keep you company.'

'Well I'll be all right,' said Nick, politely trying not to sound discouraging and, to his disappointment, succeeding.

The first train was to Bank. 'That's OK,' said Duncan, as Nick knew he would, 'I'll get the Central line from Bank to Mile End and change there.'

It soon came buzzing along the tracks, smugly looking down on the ugliness either side of the railway arches. If a

Docklands Light Railway train could talk it would shade the East End in with contempt, and hum in high tension tones how glad it was to glide above the grim and grimy habitat of mankind. 'Too base, my dear, too base.' Although in truth it could only flash little messages on an electronic display box, repeating again and again 'Green Route' and 'Bank' for the benefit of forgetful tube travellers. And it was Nick who looked back, in anger, at his chosen home, forcing himself to recall why he had forsaken leaves and frisky lambs for this urban life of his.

'I'm thinking,' said Duncan, perhaps so that Nick might be certain, 'it would be better to walk through to Monument and get on the District line there.'

'Probably,' said Nick.

He had once, on a tube platform, spotted a sweet wrapper (really they were odd things to be thinking about) that looked, from where he stood, just like a tiny walrus. Tusks, flippers, perfectly formed by some careless twist and toss of the fingers, although when he had picked it up the resemblance had collapsed at once into crumpledness. But the funny thing had been that, when he threw it down again, some colossal employee of LRT, not entirely unlike a walrus themselves, had lolloped over, flattened limbs hauling the uniformed blubber across the platform, an androgynous tenor protesting loudly of Nick's irresponsible littering of the London Underground.

All this drabness of existence could be swept up and burned. With energy, with fire. His energy, his fire. That was why he had come, no?

'Here we go,' said Duncan, childlike.

Mute Docklands Light Railway trains on the Green Route to Bank treat their passengers to a moment of high absurdity when they plunge, much as the proverbial ferret, down a steep incline and into the ground. Hades bearing Persephone into the chasm of hell, as Nick had once put it. Ye who enter here abandon hope. Though Nick clung to hope as if it were one of the chrome handrails of the train. All these thoughts of his, clinging Nick whose patriarch was dead, seized and borne into the earth, no, burned to ashes it was to be (scraped up potash sprinkled about Dorothy Floribunda). Nick could anchor nothing of this. He had lost even a sense of loss. He was numb.

'I like that bit,' said Duncan.

'Yes,' said Nick, sniffing out half a laugh.

This tortuous progress, through the clogged, choked city, with its snarled traffic and snarling travellers, its sickly air that blackened the water he washed his face in and bred tiny blackheads on his forehead, this progress – he was breathing soup, thick soup, it would take him hours, days perhaps, to wade through it to journey's end, journey's beginning, all change for the Intercity to Shrewsbury. Wading through this London that he loved.

'So,' said Duncan. They had left the train and followed the tiled subways to the parting of Eastbound and Westbound. 'Look, I'll give you my phone number and then when you get back . . .' He rested light but hateful fingertips on Nick's elbow. 'I'm so sorry about your grandfather. I don't know what to say really. If there's anything – '

'That's all right.'

Duncan pursed his lips and blew through his nose, shaking his head. 'Give me a call when you get back, eh?' he said, as if it were a great sacrifice on his part. Which, in fairness, it might well have been.

Neither of them had a pen, but Duncan found an eager American family on the Westbound platform who between them had about thirty. He scribbled his own number on the back of a receipt, then insisted on Nick giving him his. And then, with that strangest of handshakes that passes between two strangers who have just spent the night swapping orgasms and are now restrained by public decency, Duncan went. And to Nick's relief, a train west arrived before he emerged on the opposite platform.

'That's that,' he said quietly to himself.

And repeated it when he found himself alone at last, in the tumult of London's focal point, Trafalgar Square, freezing cold, hunched up on one of the stone seats and watching the fountains warily in case the spray from them blew his way. I am Nick Thomas, assistant news editor of *Gayweek*, paid up member (annual) of Friends of the Earth and contact lens wearer. And that is the world. 'That's that.'

'Beg pardon,' said the fulsome lady who sat by Nick puffing square yards of coat and waterproof. She had a North Welsh accent, and had been singing all the while in her native tongue to her husband, ugly of face and wrapped in ugly clothes; though Nick had not noticed, for he was used to hearing Welsh spoken, he had heard it often in Shrewsbury, especially at the Show.

'Sorry?'

'I thought you said something?'

'Oh. No.'

'Nice the weather, isn't it?' said the Welsh lady, who did not understand the unconversational codes of London. 'Not what you'd expect for November at all.'

'No,' said Nick, smiling politely but thinking to glance at his watch in preparation for an escape. He had a Welsh second cousin.

'Bit chilly, mind. It's like I said just this morning. The sun looks lovely, but when it goes in it's as cold as anything.'

'Yes,' said Nick, and although there had been times when he had sat in Trafalgar Square and wished with all his might that somebody, anybody, would talk to him, he remembered them not now, for now was now and then had been then. And now he wanted no-one.

'I'm sorry,' he said, standing. 'I'm afraid I have to meet some friends.'

'Oh, goodbye then,' said the Welsh lady, and her husband too grunted something.

'Nice talking to you,' said Nick.

But then, as he turned, Nick saw Duncan, the body, standing near the Column in a patch of pigeons. And Duncan had seen Nick. And he was waving to catch his attention. And in his confusion Nick kept turning, as if he had failed to spot Duncan – but only after a pause that was sure to have been noticed – completing in this way a full circle on the spot and coming to face the Welsh lady once more.

'Except,' he blurted, 'do you know what time it is?' Then added: 'I rather think my watch may be wrong.'

'It's ten past eleven,' said the Welsh lady's Welsh husband in his gruff Welsh voice.

'Oh,' said Nick. 'Then I don't have to be there yet.' He sat again, fixing his eyes intently on the Welsh lady, but only in order to avoid looking out across the Square.

'Oh well then,' said the lady. 'That's nice. You know, it's funny, you know, nobody in this city talks very much. I hope you don't mind me saying so. Are you from London?'

'No,' said Nick. 'Yes. Yes. I live here, yes. But I'm from Shrewsbury.'

'Oh,' – turning to her husband – 'Did you hear that? Shrewsbury,' – and back to Nick – 'Almost from Wales then! We're from Wales, see, but I expect you've guessed that.' She laughed. 'We're very fond of Shrewsbury though. We always go to the Show. Every year since 1963 we've been. Missed it then because of my mother. Well, she was very poorly at the time, see, I didn't like to leave her, though she lived to Christmas you know. But we've been ever since. We live in Dolgellau.'

'Right,' said Nick, the mention of death passing him by

completely in his state of agitation.

'Have you ever been to Dolgellau?'

'No. Well, I think I may have been through it. We used to go to Barmouth sometimes when I was a boy.'

'Barmouth? Abermoudac you should say, you know,' – again she laughed – 'No, but we like the English, don't we?' She barely even turned to her husband to acknowledge his incorporation in the pronoun. 'You'd like Dolgellau. But Abermoudac is nice, yes. We've lived in Dolgellau since we were married you know. Thirty-two years that is. And we thought we'd better see London once, but we wouldn't want to live here. And Cardiff we go to now and then – my cousin is down there, see? He works in the docks. And all round you know – over to England, to Shrewsbury, and Chester we like, don't we? Yes though, it's a lovely town Shrewsbury. I expect you miss it don't you.'

Not a bit, thought Nick, but he nodded and said 'Yes.'

'And do you like London?'

'Actually,' said Nick, and still he had not the courage to look if Duncan was there waving, or even walking towards him, 'I do, yes.'

'To live in?'

'Yes.'

'Oh, we wouldn't want that, would we? No, don't like the pace, see. Everyone rushing, nobody talking.' She laughed – rather she laughed always, as she spoke, but sometimes, such as now, the laughter swept the words aside completely. 'I like talking, see. I expect you noticed. Talk too much, my husband says I do. That's the Welsh for you though, isn't it? No, but it's nice to chat to somebody. That's what I wouldn't like. But you say you like it?'

'Yes,' said Nick, summoning enough pluck at last to look round. Duncan, of course, had taken the hint and gone. 'Yes,' he said again, drawing the word out as he scanned the Square for any sign of the offending body. 'I like it here,' – turning back – 'there's lots happening. A lot more than back home. Back in Shrewsbury I mean. I don't think I'd want to go back there really.'

'Oh,' said the Welsh lady, having not one single idea what Nick could be talking about. 'Oh well, I suppose for you youngsters, you know, but we're a bit older really. We find plenty to do, you know. And we can always come for a holiday, see – well, we would have come in the summer but there's so much to do in the garden, and the weather's been all right really, hasn't it?'

'Ah,' said the husband.

'So we've managed to get round and see things. We went to have a look at the Houses of Parliament and Number Ten this morning but, well, we picked our time all right. You heard the news though?'

Nick stared at her in surprise, and for the first time in their conversation she entered into his consciousness wholly, her pincushion cheeks tucked into the corners of her broad and grinning mouth, her eyes stiched like button bright press studs into the copious fabric of her face. A raggy doll of a woman, all stuffed with humanity, and Nick began to say yes, it would be so good to say yes, yes, he had heard the news. Yes, his grandfather, whom he had once known how to love, was dead, and he had not even been paying attention.

But the Welsh lady spoke first.

'Mrs Thatcher has resigned,' she explained. 'Never thought she'd go now myself. Not after the other day, but, apparently she decided this morning, see, so you can imagine, the place is like bedlam, reporters everywhere.'

'She's resigned?' said Nick. 'You mean, she's gone?'

'Yes, hard to believe after all this time, isn't it. Good riddance to her I say. Although I don't know, if this business in the Gulf gets much worse. You need strong leaders in wartime, see, like Churchill was. And she's certainly strong.'

'She's gone,' repeated Nick. It had suddenly become very apparent to him that everyone in Trafalgar Square was smiling and laughing, that the sun was too bright for an ordinary November day, that the taxis and buses were blowing their horns and revving their engines in a cheery sort of way. And, at arm's length from himself, he could tell he was smiling, about to say how pleased he was, smiling and nodding and thinking well wasn't that just wonderful, wasn't that just the best piece of news he had had in ages, they could devote a special issue of the paper to it, real news at last, Clara would laugh, she would say, 'Real news for you Nick,' she had even said something about a supplement the week before, if it happened. Which it had. Which was wonderful.

But he saw all this in himself from an odd distance, because he already had news to contend with. And it was time to leave all this, move on. He didn't know if he meant Trafalgar Square or everything, or if they weren't the same anyway. But it was time to advance.

He looked at his watch without bothering to check the time. 'Maggie out, eh? I'm afraid I've got to be off though, I'm sorry. It was nice talking to you.'

'Oh yes, lovely,' said the Welsh woman, beaming all over her magnificent face. 'Maybe we'll see you in Shrewsbury sometime, you never know. Are you back there often?'

'Almost never.'

'Oh well, well it was lovely talking to you. Goodbye.'

'Goodbye.'

As he walked away Nick heard the Welsh lady's husband, who evidently used his voice so infrequently he had forgotten that other people could hear it, saying: 'Nice lad that, but I'm buggered if I know why he wants to live here.'

Joanne Gooding

Interior designs

Damn. What a God-damn awful, one-damn-thing-after-another sort of day it had been. Sally dragged her overnight bag from the clutter on the back seat of the car, hauled it and herself out, locked up and crunched her way through the gravel to the front door of Whitelady House.

The brass bell-push gleamed next to a discreet sign which whispered rather than proclaimed, 'Bed and Breakfast,' and the cascade of chimes had hardly ended before the door was opened by a neat, smiling, middle-aged woman.

'Mrs Summer?' The woman nodded, smiling a little less as she shook Sally's offered hand. 'I'm – '

'Miss Johnson,' Mrs Summer interrupted her. 'You're Rosemary's friend, aren't you? I'm pleased to meet you.' She didn't sound pleased and Sally thought that Mrs Summer was probably one of those women who liked punctuality. She certainly looked like one of those women. Bad start. Ah well, after a day like today, what else could she expect?

'I'm sorry I'm late.'

'That's all right.' Mrs Summer stepped back and held the door wide. 'Do come in.'

'I've been driving around for *hours*. I mean, you wouldn't believe – '

'Didn't Rosemary draw you a map?'

'Yes she did. But honest to God, anyone would think she didn't want me to find the place. It was totally wrong.'

'Really?' Mrs Summer looked amused and Sally felt an absurd need to justify herself, resenting the cool, appraising gaze of the older woman.

'Well yes,' she said. 'It's like – she did it on purpose.' This was well over the top and Sally knew it, was embarrassed by her childish desire to blame someone else.

Mrs Summer laughed, a soft, ironic sound. 'Why would she do that?'

There was a moment of awkward silence, another moment. Sally laughed to break it – a silly, girlish giggle.

'Well,' she said. And laughed again. But now that she thought about it, Rosemary *had* given her the information about Mrs Summer's Bed and Breakfast very grudgingly. 'Why do you want to stay *there*?' she'd asked. Well, you always do, had been Sally's reply. Yes, and because Rosemary had been oh so secretive about her good old friend Mrs Summer. Sally didn't like secrets. Sally didn't like it that Rosemary had known Tom for longer than she had and that they talked, too often, about the good old days, excluding her.

Another painful silence threatened and Sally couldn't bear to laugh again, so she looked around with bright-eyed interest at the elegant hallway and staircase.

'My, my! What a lovely house!' she said. 'It's old, isn't it?'

'Very old. I'll show you around later, if you like.'

'Well, yes. That would be lovely.'

'But first, your room. If you'll follow me?'

And she led the way up the broad staircase, as the last rays of the August sun glowed through the coloured glass borders of the window on the landing, staining their clothes and skin with yellow, blue and crimson light.

Sally's room was on the first floor of the three storey house. There were five other guest rooms, but no other guests to-night. Sally wondered if the place was ever fully booked. Somehow she couldn't imagine it. Frankly, it didn't seem like a Bed and Breakfast at all. The decor, furnishings and arty bric-a-brac were definitely more in the style of a grand hotel than a country B&B. And in spite of the freshness and finish of the paintwork, the house felt uncomfortably aged. Perhaps that was just the effect of the gracious proportions and the occasional piece of very nice antique furniture; or the fact that there were Victorian pictures everywhere.

The sad, dark eyes of lovely women had watched her in the entrance hall from the paintings which hung on every wall. More soft-eyed beauties with sensual lips and voluminous hair had scrutinised her progress up the staircase; their sisters lined the corridor.

Some of the pictures were modern reproductions but most looked genuinely old, sepia prints, engravings; some familiar, the better known works of Millais and Ford Madox Brown, Burne-Jones, Rossetti; but all were of lovely women with waiting eyes. Sally began to feel a strange sense of emptiness. Hunger, no doubt. A low grumble from her stomach confirmed it. Lunch had been sparse and a long time ago.

'I wonder,' she said as they stood outside her room, 'is there anywhere I could get dinner. You don't – ?'

'Not usually.' Mrs Summer flashed her a brief, defensive look. 'There's a pub a few miles down the road. They do things in – er – baskets.'

'Nice pub?'

Mrs Summer looked pained. 'If you like dim lights and industrial disco.'

Sally didn't. 'Oh!' she said, thinking it was strange that Mrs Summer would use a word like 'industrial' to describe disco. It was the sort of thing Tom would say. Had said.

'Well . . .' Mrs Summer was softening. 'I suppose, as there are no other guests, I could make an exception. There's a pie. You could. Yes. Have supper with me. Come down to the dining room in, let's say, half an hour?'

'Oh, that's lovely. Thank you so much. And I'll just have time for a bath.' Soak away the dry dust and exhaustion of a truly rotten day.

'No!' Mrs Summer's voice came sharply and suddenly. 'No.' Calmly she repeated the word, recovering composure. 'I'm sorry. Um, we had the water cut off earlier today, and I'm afraid there was some trouble with the boiler. I mean, There's no hot water. Not enough for a bath. I'm sorry. I'll take something off the bill.'

Sally unpacked her overnight bag, brushed her hair and looked around the room. It was tastefully decorated and furnished, like everywhere else in the house, and there were pictures on all the walls. Sally had always been quite partial to the Pre-Raphaelite School, a taste Tom had teased her about: harmless stuff; sentimental, unchallenging. His inclination ran to modernist abstraction, the quick bright colours and forms of Klee and Kandinsky, the machine aesthetic of Leger, even Rothko's ineffable intensity. But then, Tom was an art historian, he understood all that.

She examined her pictures. The two she recognised were by Millais: *Autumn Leaves*, and poor Ophelia drowning in a ditch. The other three turned out to be by Millais as well. One with a distraught woman clinging to a handsome soldier who was clearly bent on leaving her: *The Black Brunswicker*. *The Romans Leaving Britain* showed a deranged-looking Celtic Princess clutching a Roman warrior; below the cliff on which she was sitting, gazing passionately out to sea, a boat waited to take her lover away. The last picture was a full-length portrait of a woman in a blue dress standing by a window. She was stretching, her back arched, hands gripped at the base of her spine and such a look of abject resignation on her face and in her stance: *Mariana*. There was a quotation from the Tennyson poem underneath the title:

. . . but most she loathed the hour
When the thick-moted sunbeam lay

Athwart the chambers, and the day
Was sloping towards his western bower.
Then she said, 'I am very dreary,
He will not come,' she said;
She wept, 'I am aweary, weary,
Oh God, that I were dead!'

Sally felt empty again. She glanced quickly around the room, suddenly irritated by the women in the pictures. They all looked so bloody miserable, even the girls in *Autumn Leaves*. She turned back to *Mariana* and could almost hear the rustle of the blue dress and the crick of vertebrae and a weary groan that caught on and changed into a sob of despair.

No. That was a real sound. Not imagined. A sudden night wind stirring the leaves on the tree outside the window. She turned quickly. It was dark now. She crossed the room to close the curtains. There was another groan, from her stomach this time.

Then she got an absolute conviction that someone was standing behind her. A still presence, a sense, more than a sound, of someone breathing and eyes watching: passionate eyes, bereft of hope, of anything – except intensity.

Jesus Christ! But she was tired. Cold, tired, hungry and a little spaced out. She'd be seeing things next!

From the kitchen downstairs a wholesome smell of cooking came shimmying up the staircase and under her door. It was nearly time to go down. Yes, she would go down. The room was oppressing her. It was so cold. Icy.

*

Mrs Summer turned from the stove as Sally came into the kitchen. 'Almost ready,' she said. 'Go on through.' She nodded towards the narrow door that opened onto her private dining room. 'I'll be with you in a tick.'

Two places had been set at the polished mahogany table:
linen napkins in silver rings, two glasses each, side plates, a
basket of bread rolls. A bottle of mineral water and one of
rather good red wine flanked the flower arrangement that was
the table's centrepiece. Sally sat down and poured herself a
glass of water. Not glass, crystal. Mrs Summer did things in
style.

Sally sipped her water, leaned back in her chair and closed
her eyes. She was dog tired. Exhausted. It had come on so suddenly too. Sometimes it happened like that. You can only push
yourself so far, running on empty, then the body and brain
have had enough. 'Death is nature's way of telling you to slow
down.' She smiled at the old joke; but really, it wasn't all that
funny.

Sally opened her eyes and found herself gazing at the wall
opposite and another reproduction of *Mariana*. It was larger
than the one in her room and the colours looked brighter.
Christ! It was cold in the dining room, too. She put down her
glass with a hand that noticeably wobbled. Damn it! She'd let
her blood sugars get too low. She had to eat something. And
change places; she didn't relish the thought of staring at
Mariana through supper. She had it in her to hate that bloody
painting.

She was getting to her feet when Mrs Summer appeared
with the food.

'No, no, sit down. I can manage!'

And then it was just too silly to ask to swap places.

'You seem a bit peaky,' said Mrs Summer as she served the
meal.

'Just tired.' Sally managed a limp smile.

'Have some wine. This is strong full-bodied stuff. Good
for anaemia. You do look pale.'

'It's been a long day.'

'And some more broccoli? Plenty of iron in that.'

'Thank you.'

'So.' Mrs Summer got comfortable and forked up some dinner. 'What brings you to this neck of the woods?'

And over the meal Sally told her about the job and the travelling and the meeting she'd had that morning with a supplier; and Mrs Summers listened with such careful attention that Sally found herself talking about Tom, that she was on the way to spend the weekend with – how should she call him – ? Not boyfriend, that was a silly way to describe a man of fifty, and man-friend sounded so awful. Lover? Such a tacky ring to it. She settled for 'Er,' and a pause, and 'friend,' with particular emphasis.

Mrs Summer caught on right enough. 'How long have you known him?'

'Five years.' Dear God! Was it really that long?

'And you don't want to get married?'

'Well !' How much meaning could be got into one word?

Mrs Summer nodded and sipped her wine. 'He's not the marrying kind?'

'He *was* married. Once.'

'But he left her.'

It was more a statement than question but Sally confirmed it.

'For you.' Statement again. It suddenly occurred to Sally that Mrs Summer knew all about her. Rosemary, the bitch, must have told her. And did Mrs Summer know Tom? For sure she did. Bloody hell!

Sally felt her cheeks burning and a slight sweat on her forehead. Was it hot in the room? It seemed hot. Or was she sickening for something?

'I'm sorry,' she whispered. She wasn't embarrassed, was she? She'd never been embarrassed by it before. Sure, Tom had left his wife, but it hadn't been *her* fault. She hadn't even known he was married, that first time.

'Don't apologise to me, dear,' Mrs Summer said quietly. 'I'm sure it wasn't your fault.'

'No. I didn't mean . . . I mean, I don't feel all that . . .'

'Have some more wine.'

'Yes. Thank you.' She looked up to where *Mariana* stretched out her boredom. Yes, it was time to change the subject. 'Your pictures,' she said, intending to tell Mrs Summer how much she liked them, but a sudden sense of aversion intervened. 'They're rather depressing!'

Mrs Summer glanced round with a light laugh. From every wall, they gazed their stricken gazes, the eyes of abandoned women. Yes. That's what they were. All of them. Abandoned.

'I suppose so,' Mrs Summer said. 'A lot of them were already here when I bought the house. To be honest, I'm a bit sick of them myself. But Sylvia likes them.'

'Sylvia? Your daughter?'

'No, no. Heavens no! I don't have any children. Sylvia used to live here, oh, ages ago.'

'How long?'

'Hundred years? Mrs Summer was guessing. 'Yes it must be about that.'

'I'm sorry, I don't – ?'

'My ghost, you see.'

'Ghost?'

'Didn't Rosemary tell you? I thought everyone knew about my ghost. Died for love, poor thing.' She sighed and added as a sort of vague afterthought, 'Killed for it too.'

'What happened?'

'Usual story. The man she loved abandoned her for someone else. She killed the other woman. Isn't it strange, that habit of blaming the other woman? Don't know why she didn't go for her old man. After all, he was the swine who deserted her.'

There was a faint tinkling of china on the dresser. 'Oops! Sorry Sylvia. Sore point.' The china settled down. 'Anyway. After that, she killed herself.'

'In this house?'

'Oh yes. But don't worry about the bathroom upstairs. That's not the room. Everything's got changed about over the years, you see.'

'Bathroom?'

'Oh sorry. Didn't I say? Yes. She opened her wrists up in a hot bath. Messy way to go even if it was easy to clean up.' Mrs Summer shook her head at the folly of it. 'I wouldn't. Not kill for love. And certainly not die for it. Would you?'

Sally laughed, embarrassed by the tone of the question. 'I'd rather live for it,' she said nervously.

'Wouldn't we all?' Mrs Summer raised her glass to the sentiment and drank a toast.

'But, is there *really* a ghost? Have you seen it?'

'No.' Mrs Summer pushed her empty plate aside and poured a drop more wine into her glass. 'I don't believe in ghosts.' The china resumed its shiver on the dresser. Mrs Summer turned her look towards it. 'Sometimes *that* happens, when I say or think something she wouldn't like. But it's probably just a lorry passing on the main road.'

'But you said there are things she doesn't like and does like. I mean, the pictures?'

'Just my fancy.' Mrs Summer grinned and her eyes glinted as they caught the light. 'You know, old ladies living on their own get funny ideas.'

'You're not so old.' Not much older than Tom. Come to think of it, probably not as old as Tom.

Mrs Summer's head dipped briefly in acknowledgement of the compliment. 'It's rather like the way small children sometimes have an invisible friend they tell their secrets to. Some-

times I like to think she's here. I natter to her and imagine re-
sponses. It's a good way of pretending I don't talk to myself.'

'She's friendly, then, your ghost? I mean, not hostile?'

'Not hostile to me.'

*

Sally undressed on autopilot, methodically hanging up and
folding her clothes. She slipped into her cotton robe, tucked
her feet into her slippers and padded off to the bathroom. The
house seemed very large and very empty. Dim night-lights
glowed over the landing and stairs, just enough to see by. It
was deathly quiet. Somewhere, far away in the dark depths of
the house, a clock was marking off the seconds. No sound
from the main road. They could have been on the moon for all
the outside world made its presence felt. No sounds but the
sounds old houses make when their walls cool down in the
night air and tired joists settle on weathered stone with small,
occasional sighs and clicks.

The air in the bathroom felt particularly moist and chill and
Sally shivered as she brushed her teeth over the ornate porcelain sink. It was a very old sink, its blue maker's mark and
scroll were faded and illegible, its glaze crazed around the
thick moulding of the overflow. The bath was old too, a great
cast iron thing with clawed feet, deep and narrow like a white
sarcophagus. Perhaps this was not the original bathroom; but
Sally couldn't help wondering if that was *the* bath. She found
herself glancing at it out of the corner of her eye and wondering why Mrs Summer had said she couldn't have a bath. The
water seemed hot enough now. And then telling her all that rot
about the ghost. Trying to freak her out. Well, she wouldn't
get freaked out. Sod that.

Although it was easy, in the still emptiness of the old house,
to imagine things . . . even though Tom was always telling her

how unimaginative she was. He would laugh if he could see her now, shaking and quaking in her cotton gown, which was far too thin to keep out the damp caresses of the cold. She turned off the tap. The water pipes growled and vibrated for a few moments, but even after they were still, there came from them a faint singing sound, like a noise coaxed from the rim of a fine wine glass. The note seemed to rise in pitch as it faded, so that when Sally wasn't even sure if she could hear it or not, her ears hurt and she put up her hands to block the sound or the echo of it oscillating.

And then she felt faint; suddenly hot and flushed and terribly faint. She gripped the basin as her thighs trembled and her knees collapsed while her head rang with a sound that wasn't there. Somehow she managed to pivot round to sit down on the broad curving lip of the bath.

She was sweating and breathing hard. She tried to calm herself. Too much red wine, that was all it was. She shouldn't drink the stuff, not after lager at lunchtime. The dizziness passed into drowsiness and she felt herself slipping, sliding over the cold enamel, backwards, downwards. She made a grab for the sink and hauled herself up, recovering her balance just in time to halt the tumble. Her mind completed the event, seeing herself fall hard against the iron base of the bath, spine cracking, head splitting.

She stood up, wiping her damp palms on her dressing gown, forcing herself to laugh. *How's that for imagination, Tom!* But it wasn't funny. That bath wasn't funny.

Sally was relieved to get back to her room. There had been no mishaps along the corridor, thank God. No dizzy spells. But she was so tired. Bone weary. She stretched and yawned, her spine arching and aching. Her hands gripped the small of her back to give it some ease. Out of the corner of her eye she saw *Mariana* reflecting her pose with something like mockery. She shook herself out of it. Damn painting! She'd turn

the damn thing to the wall. Sally marched up to it, determined
to do just that; but the picture wasn't hanging, it was fixed with
mirror plates, screwed tight. There was no shifting it. She'd
put something over it, then. She pulled one of the pillows out
of its case and hung the slip over the painting, making sure to
wedge the corners securely in place behind the frame. *Good fit.
Yes, very nice. That's sorted you, you miserable bitch!*

Behind Sally, it seemed that someone sighed.

The wind in the trees, just the wind in the trees and tired-
ness and too much to drink. She switched the bedside light on
and the overhead light off and got into bed in her dressing
gown. She had no nightdress and it was far too cold to sleep in
the raw. Too cold for August. How could it be August and be
so cold? Her skin felt as cold as cast iron. She reached out a
goose-fleshed arm to switch off the light and snuggled down,
curled up to get warm, her body folded away from the chill
empty spaces under the sheet.

She was longing for sleep, hungry for it. Yes, she felt terribly empty, starved. She couldn't be hungry, not after that
wonderful supper. But she felt it – a deep ravenous need,
wanting, just wanting, craving. Something. Cigarette? Anything. She switched on the light, the sudden brightness hurt-
ing her eyes.

There was a cut glass ashtray on the bedside table. Good.
Mrs Summer didn't object to smoking then. Although the
cheapness of the ashtray compared with everything else in the
house seemed to suggest she didn't rate it very highly either.

Sally's bag was just within reach. She was glad about that
because she didn't really have the energy to get out of bed. She
found her cigarettes and groped around in the rattling depth
of the bag for her lighter. Pencils, pens, lipstick cases, house
keys, car keys, cheque book, a packet of tissues, purse, her
other purse. Where was it? In frustration, she tipped the bag
out onto the floor. There it was. She rescued the lighter and

scooped everything else back into the bag.

The first puff of the cigarette made her feel sick. She persevered and her head went mushy. No. It was no good. She was feeling really faint again. She stubbed out the cigarette, switched off the light and lay back against the pillows, staring into the dark of the room.

A light rectangle glimmered dimly from the wall facing the bed: the pillowslip under which she had tucked *Mariana* up for the night. It made it worse somehow. The other pictures had melted into darkness; but this one intruded by its absence, demanding her attention. She should take the cover off. She would – but she felt too tired, too weak to move. Really weak. Drained. Her eyes closed and her body seemed to be floating away from her – or was that just her life streaming out, flowing thickly and thinly diluting in hot red water?

She was woken by a sharp creak on the stairs. Someone creeping, step after step on the thick carpet, coming up. Then there was a faint glow from the corridor, seeping under the door, passing, fading as the soft tread passed and faded through a rustle of fabric.

Sally sat up and flicked on the light. She was fully awake, her body rigid, senses straining. Distantly, on the edge of hearing, came the tinkle of china from the dresser downstairs, and then the rough, full-throated roar of a juggernaut passing along the main road. The real sound was comforting in its late twentieth century banality. Sally relaxed against the pillows. She was making a fool of herself. Strange house, strange noises, allowing herself to get spooked by a story that Mrs Summer took quite lightly. But her heart was pounding and when the floorboards overhead groaned under gentle footfall, she was truly scared. She sat up again, bolt upright, staring ahead at the wall facing the bed, at the picture of Mariana and the pillowslip in a crumpled heap on the floor below it – too far from the wall.

Sally leapt out of bed in a rush of fear-powered adrenalin. She was across the room in moments and clutching the pillowslip, touching the corners which were creased and grimed from being rammed behind the frame. And one corner was ripped, a fresh ragged tear and she glanced up at the picture to see there were threads still clinging where they'd caught on a screw.

The pillowslip fell from her hands.

Outside the window the trees sighed and moaned. No, not outside. The sigh was inside the room – a room Sally would not stay in for one second longer than she had to. She had to get out. She'd drive somewhere, anywhere, sleep in a lay-by . . . . The china tinkled like laughter in the room below. But this time no juggernaut heaved through the night.

She dressed quickly and packed her bag. I'm going, I'm going, she muttered. Just let me be. Got everything? Yes. Her hands shook as she scrawled out a cheque. How much should she add for the meal? Ten pounds? Twenty pounds? What did it matter as long as she got out!

Car keys? Where were they? Not in her bag. Pockets? No. Had they spilled out when she'd emptied her bag? She groped under the bed and the bedside table. In her car then? Yes, she must have left them in the ignition.

There was another groan – almost a howl – and Sally fled from the room. The nightlights on the landing weren't on and she couldn't find the switch. But the moonlight from outside was just enough to find her way by. She staggered to the top of the stairs, then down gripping the banister rail. The red stained glass in the windows cast pools of dark carmine which splashed over her coat as she stumbled downstairs.

Half way down, a step creaked loudly under her foot – and when she got to the bottom it creaked again under no foot.

Then she was outside on the gravel path with the door shut

behind her. Light flooded the front of the house as she triggered the security cell. Sally got to her car. It was locked.

Mrs Summer, alarmed by the lights, found Sally weeping and shaking and emptying her bag onto the car bonnet.

'What's happening?'

Sally couldn't answer, but then there were strong arms supporting her and she was sobbing and laughing, shuddering fit to fall apart and babbling the whole story while Mrs Summer took her back into the house.

In the warm sanctuary of the kitchen, Sally drank hot chocolate stiff with brandy and Mrs Summer calmly explained how the old chimneys made noises and yes, they did sound strange and terribly close sometimes, and it was true that she herself had gone upstairs to check the windows and that was what Sally must have heard.

'I feel so stupid,' Sally confessed. Mrs Summer nodded unsmilingly.

But the car keys had definitely gone.

'They'll turn up in the morning,' Mrs Summer assured her, as she took Sally back to her room. 'Get some sleep now,' her eyes looked mocking, 'or you won't be your best for poor Tom tomorrow.'

'I'll never sleep.'

'You'll sleep.'

Sally felt heavy, a stone effigy laid out on the mattress. Her head sinking down, down into the pillow. She couldn't move. *You'll sleep.* Something had happened. *You won't be your best for poor Tom.* Something bad was happening, now, in her brain and her body, squeezing her life out. Of course. No ghost. There was no ghost at all; just a mad, obsessive woman, an abandoned bitch who relished the role of the victim, surrounded herself with images of loss and desertion. Tom's wife.

Oh yes. And Rosemary knew, had tried to stop her coming

to a house filled with a monstrous desire for revenge. And the warm milk, laced with brandy, had been spiked with something else. For sure. And Sally was slipping, slipping slowly, relentlessly into that black hole of darkness that lets nothing out.

Becky Summer sat up all night in the dining room – which had once been a bathroom – and smiled at the dresser where the china trembled and rattled. She had known, as soon as she saw her, that this Sally Johnson was *the* Sally Johnson, the one for whom Tom had left her. Well, we had to meet someday, she thought. And how did she feel about it? Becky nodded and her smile deepened. She felt just fine, thanks. Absolutely fine. She chuckled softly at the thought of how hard it was going to be to wake the poor girl from her drugged sleep. But it was better that way.

'You shouldn't have come here.'

Sally's eyes stung open to white glare as the curtains were swished aside. Her tongue felt too big and so sticky, clamped to the roof of her mouth. She sat up awkwardly, supporting her weight on her elbows, blinking and stupid. Mrs Summer stood by the window, a blurred silhouette against the sharp dazzle, insubstantial as sunlight. She moved to a shadowed part of the room and Sally's eyes followed. Mrs Summer's lips parted again. 'You shouldn't have come.' Was she smiling? 'It's not safe for you here.'

'You . . .' said Sally, voice croaking.

'No.'

Breakfast passed without incident, both women watchful; but there was little to say. Becky was tired but she knew she had to stay alert until Sally was safely away. There was one last attempt. Coming downstairs for the last time, Sally stumbled and nearly went headlong. But Becky had expected something like that and was there just in time to steady her.

'Someone *pushed* me!' Sally's panicky look was accusing.

'Carpet's a bit loose.' Becky Summer smiled and escorted Sally out of the house.

As Becky watched her drive away, she had one moment of envy – fierce, brief – then it was gone and with it went Sylvia's approval. China broke in the kitchen when Becky washed up. 'Don't be spiteful!'

As she ran her morning bath, Becky wondered how far Sylvia's influence extended. There were some nasty corners en route to the motorway and it was starting to drizzle. After weeks of dry weather the motorway would be greasy. And Sylvia was angry, more angry than Becky had known her before. She'd been cheated out of revenge. Poor Sylvia. She'd died in anger and could never move on. They'd grown apart, through the years. Sad really. They'd had so much to share in the early days. Both of them bitter. But in a curious way it seemed that Sylvia had absorbed all her rage and resentment, fed on it, drained it away. 'And now you're angry with me! You think I've betrayed you.' Maybe she had. It had been a testing time, this confrontation with Sally. But Becky had passed. Passed on. She knew now that all the resentment and bitterness had finally gone.

Sally drove carefully, quite slowly in spite of her need to put distance between her and that house. She was still scared, but telling herself it was all right now, it was over and she'd never go back there. She was safe – but quite sleepy in spite of the strong coffee Mrs Summer had insisted she drink.

Too sleepy. The blare of a horn and a rush as a lorry passed by too close shook her to her senses. 'My God! I dropped off there!' It was the second near miss that morning. Coming round a sharp bend on the road to the motorway she had nearly gone head-on into an oncoming car.

This wasn't like her at all. She should get off the road. Have a sleep perhaps. The night hadn't been peaceful.

She took the next exit and pulled over onto a grass verge. Was it safe there? she wondered. The bend was quite sharp. Too bad. She couldn't fight it any longer. Tired. So tired.

As Sally nestled her head down and closed her eyes, Becky Summer dozed in her bath. The water was hot and deep and comforting. She felt peaceful and sure now that Sylvia had at last given up. She sighed and lay back, letting her head sink into the warmth, felt the hands, oh so tender, pressing down on her shoulders. 'Now, Sylvia,' she thought, 'none of your tricks!' But the hands were insistent as the water closed over her face and she struggled and kicked as her hair floated up and the strong, gentle hands pushed irresistibly, holding her down.

Katherine Eban Finkelstein

Mortal Taste

from *Mortal Taste*

Penelope has been alone before, alone for hours and days. She can circle the house like a sliver of moon, and throw light into the recesses of unused rooms. She can make pillows out of crushed velvet, or pale flowered pink. She can turn on all the lights in her make-up mirror and outline her lips in orange, pencil in a beauty mark, and tie lace in her hair. She sprays perfume in her stocking drawer, where shining nylon legs are tangled. A purple garter belt peeks out from under velcro shoulder pads. A woman's life in a drawer.

When she can barely move with sadness, still Penelope looks in the make-up mirror and draws mascara through her lashes. And yet as she reclines on her pillowed chair, tears blacken her cheeks in tracks.

'Penelope, look at the moon.'

Penelope drops her blush on the counter. Chips of color shatter.

'I was just watching you put on make-up. You're doing a terrible job, sweetheart. Give all that up unless you want me to do it for you, and look at the moon.'

Penelope points a wet and frightened face towards the empty bedroom. Dampened make-up is streaked along her jaw bone, and towards the cleft in her chin.

'I'm serious. We women have a lot to learn from nature. The moon is only a piece of silver, but its light fills the entire sky. That's the effect you want on your face.'

'Oh please.' Penelope speaks aloud when she hears the strange voice, and tries to calm herself. 'I am not so alone here. I have an evening to myself.' She sips from the champagne glass, into which she has poured a yogurt drink. 'What a luxury. What a luxury,' she sips again. 'Luxury.' She repeats the word as if, by saying it, something fragrant or quilted will appear at her feet; as if, by saying it, the ceiling will vanish, revealing an infinite sky.

The stars are cast out like sugared sweets. The evening is a living blue. The blues are like waves calling out from a cove. The night springs up like words, the ones she keeps on hearing.

Her skin is soft. She dabs at it with a Q-tip. 'I am young.' The thought is cheerful.

The bedroom is dark. The spreading robe on her bed glows like peaches, a fruit still-life on a transformed table. She wants food. She wonders, is it safe to balance on the backyard fence, and eat apples under that sliver of moon? Silver and red are her colors.

Darron's colleague once told her this at their Christmas party, as she continued looping tinsel on branches. 'If I may say so, silver and red are your colors.' Across the room Darron rolls wine corks in glitter, and heaps them in a salad bowl. Guests stand in the hallway. 'Why, thank you.' She straightens her slipping Santa cap, and handles the pine with trembling fingers. 'It's rather hot in here, don't you think? Could I trouble you to open the window?' She gestures to the frosted pane. She could be eating snow. Her stockings might ice over. Her toes could disappear into soil. She could be sinking into winter. Her breath creates shapes in sub zero weather. She must serve a platter of imported cheeses. Darron winks at her as she's falling over couches. 'So sorry.' She is headed for the door again. Branches wave in the opening garden. The snow is crisp. The only thing she's biting into is night time. Mushrooms stuffed with crab meat recede, and she's left alone with hope. Her hands are red with sangria.

She hears the voice from the bedroom again.

'You're not so alone, but a night in this house is not such a luxury. I know what a luxury is, believe me, and this is not it. You don't have to pretend you're happy. Don't believe these people who tell you what happiness is. Exercise some skepticism. You fool yourself so badly, it's going to start rubbing off on me, the longer I lie here. Let's go back to the moon idea. God only knows what you're doing to your face.'

Penelope puts down her mascara wand and looks into the bedroom again. She wants silence from the evening, that is all she wants. She is fixing her face for when Darron comes back with his mother.

'I will not be ignored by you. I'm much more assertive than I used to be, Penelope. No one enacts their horrible rituals on me any more, so you can't shut me out like a freakish voice. I know you're lonely. Walk in here and sit down. And bring your make-up with you.'

Penelope picks up the striped case and peers from the archway. 'Who's there? Hello?' She waits for a response. 'Hello?' She edges into the room. 'Is someone there?' The darkness strains her eyes. A heavy drape drifts from the window.

She is used to hearing voices. Even when she turns on her brights and swings off the highway, she thinks she can hear Sirens, half-women, half-fish. Her package of salmon on the passenger seat is wrapped and taped. Salmon is her best fish, with french-fried potatoes and a salad of numerous, vinegared greens. 'I'm not stopping for you, or anyone,' she says to the singing women. She smiles to herself on the high seat of Darron's land rover.

The bedroom is flooded with brilliant moonshine. The moon is a fruit suspended in an edible constellation of light.

'This is not your imagination. Surprised?' Lying amidst pillows on the bed is her old friend Cindy Baberneck.

'Cindy!' Penelope cries out, falling against the window. 'What can you possibly be doing here?' She begins to cry. 'Oh please. I'm so scared.'

'I don't like being lumped with all your other tragedies. Can I smoke in here?' Cindy takes out a golden package from within the folds of her jacket.

'Oh God, do what you want.' Penelope sinks to the floor, crying.

'I've come to visit, Penelope, looking lovely for you to boot. Why do you want to ruin our special time together?'

'I'm tired Cindy. I thought you were only in the restaurant.'

'Penelope, please. I love you. That's why I came back.'

'What do you mean, came back? Where have you been? I don't believe you. I'm going to throw a pillow at you.'

'Calm down. I can move around, you know. It's not like I'm chained to a burning lake, or stuck in a bad restaurant for all eternity. I can come and go as I please. And don't throw anything at me. I couldn't defend myself and you know that. I'm very weak. And I'm smoking. Do you want to set the room on fire?' Cindy shrugs. 'I'm wearing my smoking jacket. Always. Always I'm well dressed. What a good feeling that is.' She smiles at Penelope. 'Just enjoy my visit for what it's worth.'

'I feel sick.'

'You don't look too good. But I think we can fix that with a little make-up.'

'With a little make-up? You're going to put my whole life right with cosmetics? And who are you to be putting anything right, after you cursed me out, and left me? And with what you did to yourself in the end . . .'

'We're not talking about that tonight, do you understand? Or I'm leaving. Not a word on that subject.' Cindy sits up in bed. The lapels of her jacket fall away to reveal a golden bustiere. 'We can talk about that on another visit. No questions tonight or I'm gone, like I was never here at all. I have a few things I may share with you, if I feel like it.' She purses her lips and looks for an ashtray. 'Let's limit the thrust of this visit to cosmetic application. And get me an ashtray, would you?'

Penelope gets to her knees, brushing the hair from her face.

'And bring along some make-up remover. I'm so excited to see you. You know,' Cindy calls to her in the bathroom, 'I always dress appropriately. Better than appropriately. Perfectly. But you keep the house so cold. Who could have been prepared for this? I'm going to have to borrow a sweater, or at least put on some heat. And why are you looking so terrible? Who is taking care of you these days? Do you like this smoking jacket?'

Penelope reappears with a box of tissues, some facial cleanser, and a jade ashtray. She switches on a bedside lamp to see Cindy more clearly. The smoking jacket is a rich black velvet, stitched with satin the pattern of leaves. The buttons are also like little green leaves. She wears sheer harem pants that float in a triangle across the bed. Her stockings sparkle in the light, and her black silk shoes are thrown onto the floor. The single black ribbon pulls her hair away from the pale satisfied face.

'Aren't you a little overdressed?'

'I notice, or did when I was still in circulation, that wherever I went, the level of elegance rose accordingly. Thus I set style, Penelope. I don't capitulate to the average taste. You're alone here. What do you do for yourself when your husband leaves?'

'Not too much. I try to relax.' Every day slumbrous inactivity, and at night, those feverish imaginings.

'Let's do something with your face. First, look out your window.'

With her hands on the sill, Penelope sees the grass flattened by wind. The massive branch of the apple tree hangs over the fence. The lawn chairs swim on the deck.

'What am I looking for?' Penelope feels faint at the window, and annoyed with the project.

'Consider this a study of light.'

Penelope turns her back on the window and stares at Cindy, who is pulling out a cigarette with a thin blueing hand. 'I don't want to consider this anything. Aside from one brief encounter, we haven't seen each other in years. The last time we were together at your house, we had a terrible fight. I have a husband now, you're dead, and I don't believe you. And why are you teaching me anything? Have you grown up? I don't even know where you've been . . . wandering in the nether world, or weaving flowers in Paradise.'

Cindy shades the light from her eyes with a translucent forearm. 'I don't go out much now,' she narrows her eyes at Penelope. 'Do you remember we used to shop at Loehmann's? It was so hard, finding items of really good quality.'

'I don't care about Loehmann's, Cindy. I have serious problems.' Penelope sits down on the bed. 'It makes me nervous not to know if you're going to disappear. I don't know what you might do. I don't know what you know about me.' Here, Penelope lifts her head with curiosity, taking in the thin specter. 'Is it one of these all-knowing things?'

Cindy is sinking back into the pillows. Her pale cheek rests in the packed feathers. Her face is narrowing with concentration.

'I think a lot about death. And morbid things. Darron hates it. And I'm not really interested in them any more. I only do it to avoid my house. But he must think I'm a freak. I don't deserve him, but I would just like to be happy. Now you return from the dead and want to play with make-up. I'm not interested in playing games. I'm afraid I'm going to lose my husband.'

The black satin shifts and falls with Cindy's breathing.

'We made love for the first time in three months, and all it made me was nervous,' Penelope frowns. 'Now that I've done it, I'm going to have to keep on doing it. Who knows if he'll enjoy it. I certainly won't. And his mother is arriving.

'My palms are sweating. What good will it do me if my face is colored silver? I'll cry it all off. So I want you to go.' Penelope stands. Her face is bright with tears. 'I want you to get out of my house however you came. Don't tease me any more. I'm going into the bathroom, and when I get back you'll be gone. I hope.'

I'm sure you haven't spoken that much since we were girls. I will be seeing you.' Cindy twists her cigarette out, picks up her shoes and walks through the bedroom door.

The night remains as barren as before, the house is adrift. Penelope picks up the bag of colors and returns to her bench at the make-up mirror. With a silver eye pencil, she traces lines on her upper lids; she stencils her lips in cedar, and prefers never to speak again.

Neil Church

Parramatta

As Anne sits drinking her Monday morning coffee, she thinks about the night the two Pommie travellers came. She sees herself sitting right here on the sofa, watching the big flat-screened TV, while Julia makes a big deal of cooking something that smells pretty bad in the kitchen. There's a loud thud and the door swings open as Eddie kicks it and lumbers in. He's wearing a T-shirt with a crest and the words 'Land of Hope and Glory' on the front; the T-shirt is too small and his fat belly protrudes under it.

Eddie ignores her as usual and unhinges his big jaw to yell, 'Ju bum! Curling bum! Ze English is here! Ju bum! Welcome ze English!'

He gestures to the two figures looming behind him in the doorway, but Julia can't see him, and she doesn't come. She calls back from the kitchen,

'I'm busy, Edward.'

Eddie sings, 'Come to me, curling whirling bum.'

Julia shouts, 'Far out, Edward.'

Anne's had this for twelve months. Once she and Julia lived as bachelor girls together in the flat, getting on fine, but then a year ago Julia's yob of a Pommie boyfriend lumbered in, and ever since there's just been this continual noise of Eddie and Julia together. This is why she's glad, in a way, these two Pommies are coming to stay. Anything for a change.

Eddie met the guys when he and Julia were on holiday at Surfers' for New Year. They needed work and Eddie promised one of them a job with the building firm he works for, and invited them both to stay. Anne wasn't consulted, of course, so glad or not she sits with her arms folded, eyes fixed on the TV, as Eddie beckons them in.

She hears, 'Hi. You must be Anne? I've heard all about you.'

There's a big guy who says this and a smaller guy trailing behind, his sidekick. The accent is English, from the North of England, which seems odd because at first sight the two of them look like dinkum Aussies, in shorts and Bali T-shirts and with thongs on their brown feet. But according to Eddie they're taking a year out from Cambridge University, so she reckons there must be a bit of Pommie culture behind all that stubble.

The first thing she says to them is, 'So do yous guys hate Australia as much as Eddie does?'

The big guy says, 'Au contraire. Beats bloody Essex any day.'

She laughs and looks at Eddie, because Essex is the place Eddie comes from. Eddie give the guy a crumpled smile and says something like, 'Ee up, by gum, eckythump, when I were a lad, aye.'

The big guy turns to her with a face like Jack Benny looking into the camera in the old comedy show, like he's saying 'Who is this idiot?' Already she's thinking this guy's going to be all right.

It's Monday morning, four weeks later, and Anne finishes her coffee, and pushes the unwashed cup through the hatch into the kitchen. She thinks: four weeks ago? She leaves the flat in Macquarie Towers, goes down in the lift and out past the swimming pool and the token palm trees. Four weeks ago, he was a stranger? She turns right at the little pizza place and starts to clack her office girl heels down Parramatta Hill. Four weeks ago?

The road undulates as it descends and three humped snakes

of Fords and Holdens and Nissans slide down the hill beside her, crumpling up at the traffic lights with winking brake lights and stretching out again. It's Monday morning, a bit gone eight-forty-five. The sun is rising on its high arc from the Pacific, and Anne has to narrow her eyes against it.

Four weeks . . . Jeez. Anne hates the sun, she has hated the sun all her life, and always she curses the prickling warmth on her cheeks, the dazzling light in her eyes as she walks down Parramatta Hill. But not today. Today she feels the sunlight on her like a blessing.

Hands are shaken and Anne puts names on the Pommie strangers. Alastair, the big guy; Nick his small, shy sidekick, trailing behind him. Straight off she knows she's going to get on with Alastair the better. Not just because he's good-looking although, okay, Alastair is good-looking. Somehow she senses right away that Nick's a man's man. Although he's only small and wiry she's not surprised it's he who takes the labouring job with Eddie, and it's he who turns out to be Eddie's mate.

The labouring means Nick and Eddie getting up at half past five in the morning, and when their lives are put in tandem like this it's not surprising they turn into something of a double-act. After work they're always splashing around in the swimming pool together, or going to play snooker, or to watch cricket maybe. She remembers how once after a hard day's yakka they crawl into the flat on their hands and knees, gasping for water like dying men in the desert. This is Nick and Eddie: a pair of clowns, clowning for each other.

Meanwhile Alastair seems a bit left out. He's hurt his back bodysurfing, which is why he can't do the labouring job, and he hangs around the flat waiting for people to get back to him about bar work. He sleeps late in the mornings – she sees him still sleeping on the sofa when she goes to work, his mouth open, looking kind of sweet – and stays up late at night, watching the TV, while Nick kips on the floor. Anne starts to sit up with him: Nick doesn't mind, or doesn't wake up anyway. They play card games Alastair teaches her, or watch TV shows she's taped.

They talk, too. They talk first about Eddie and Julia.

'Eddie,' says Alastair, 'has a massive cerebellum.'

She says, 'A what?'

He says, 'His intellect is gargantuan.'

He does a little mime like his head's expanding. He and Nick both have this sarcastic way of speaking. The difference is, when Nick does it he speaks really straight so you don't know if he's being serious or not. Alastair puts on a funny voice and makes funny faces, so you know what he means, and it's funny.

'What about Julia?' she asks.

He says, 'Julia is a hyperintelligent megabeing from a distant galaxy.'

They talk seriously too. One time Alastair talks about how guilty he feels that Nick has to work the building sites and not him: they share their money, and he says he feels like a kept man. Another time she talks about her childhood in Broken Hill, and Alastair gets on to his hassles with his family at home.

He says, 'I could just stay here you know. I could just forget all of it and stay here.'

She says, 'What about Cambridge? What about your degree?'

He says, 'Fuck Cambridge.'

She probably looks nervous, like she's taken the lid off something she shouldn't, but Alastair gives her his reassuring smile, his engaging smile.

OK, so he is good looking. So he has a cleft chin like Kirk Douglas and soft brown curly hair that's receding slightly, so he looks more distinguished than you'd expect at twenty two:

so he's barrel-chested and yet slim and has well-defined muscles all over his body. So she's well aware of this. But it's the way they talk she likes.

Anne walks on into the Flinders Center. The fountain is foaming and the muzak is playing and the bright rows of chain stores are getting ready to open. This is her adult world: clean, man-made, air-conditioned. It's still good to think of this against her childhood, her mother's caravan park, Broken Hill, the unforgiving bush sun. It's good to think of what she's left behind, the bushmen with their beards and Stetsons and bare feet and tepees and ancient Holdens, with their stubbies and their cones, letting their hoarse animal cries ring out into the night. Anne always hated the bush. Most from her youth she remembers staring at endless blue air through the mossie screens in her bedroom, dreaming about civilized places, getting out.

So it's good to think how when school was finished she got the job with the travel agents, Trailblazers, in Parramatta: it was an escape, a release. OK, so Parra's not quite her dream. So the gleaming skyscrapers of the City of Sydney, the beaches, the Rocks, the Opera House, are thirty K's east down the Highway. So it was better when she and Julia were bachelor girls together, it was better when the job was new, when just to work in the cool air-conditioned office and be surrounded by people who actually wore shoes was enough. So she knows she's better than this, she'll do better than this, one day. Life amongst the Westies of the Western Suburbs is all right, but.

Anne sits at her desk with the green screen, and puts her telephone headset on, and talks to boorish, impatient guys about fortnights in Fiji and weeks in the Reef islands and weekend breaks in Alice. Half an hour of this and she's hanging out for smoko, and when smoko comes she sits with a plastic cup of coffee and listens to the cross-fire of office talk.

'This motor, since I put the V8 in, it really flies mate.'

'You didn't come to Mike's party? Oh mate, it was a rage!'

'Did you see Debbie at the disco on Saturday? She's supposed to be going with Alan but, Jeez, she starts dancing with this guy Greg – '

'Debbie! How ya going? How was your weekend?'

How was her weekend? Anne closes her eyes. She hasn't been sleeping so much this weekend.

Alastair gets his bar job in the end, not much of a job, one day and two evenings a week, and the Pommies seem to be settled in for a long stay. It's pretty crowded with the five of them in the flat, and Julia's talking about how they should split the rent five ways now, but, hell, they're all getting along pretty well. This Friday is Alastair's twenty-first birthday, and although she's known him less than four weeks, already this seems to Anne like a big occasion, almost a family occasion.

Alastair wants a rage so they go, the five of them, to the RSL Club in Surrey Hill for the disco. So they play drinking games and get seriously drunk and have a rage. Anne sees them dancing, they're all laughing together and dancing, all five of them with their arms round each other's shoulders, in a circle, dancing. And then there's Eddie and Julia dancing together, big lumbering Eddie with his spiky blond hair and English disco gear, Julia darkly Latin with a skimpy dress that used to fit her and too much make-up. Eddie's playing the clown again, putting his sunglasses on and making like he's John Travolta. And then Nick's pinching the sunglasses, little Nick with his mop of black hair and hook nose, looking a bit like Bob Dylan with the glasses on, and she and Alastair are laughing at him. She sees Alastair with his white jeans with his white boxing boots and his blue and white striped collarless shirt, a dazzling figure in the ultraviolet lights, even his teeth gleaming blue-white. She thinks: he's good to dance with; he's a real good dancer.

And once more there is the slow dance, and his arms at the small of her back, and the moment she feels his nose touch her nose, the moment when she knows they will kiss. And then there is his body against hers like a big bag of rocks, and his yeasty, animal smell; and the kissing on the dance floor; the swimming pool (Jeez, they must have been drunk), Nick and Eddie splashing about, and her body and Alastair's body, embracing, in the water, their bodies bathed in moonlight, chest-deep in water, kissing; and then her big water bed, and the warm, naked, silken darkness, in the water bed.

How was her weekend? It was like this. It was laughter in a moonlit swimming pool.

At five Anne is out on Parramatta Hill with the low sun shining in her eyes over the drive-in bottle store. Mondays are always a bind: it's a relief to reach smoko, to get to lunch, to get the first day of the week over. But even then the rest of the week stretches ahead of her, like an endless slog up the Hill beside the autos with their winking brake lights.

Always, but not today. This Monday, all is changed, like the sun which now shines in her face as a friend.

It's not like she hasn't had guys before. She's had guys, heaps of guys. It's not like she was hanging around waiting for a guy like an old spinster. It's not like, you know, a weekend spent mostly in bed with a guy is the beginning and end of what it's all about. But it's like, this time, something is there, whatever is supposed to happen has happened. This time she feels a sense of release, the same sense she had when she left Broken Hill for Parramatta. Today she thinks of the arid, silent vastness of the bush and thinks it's like the life she had, a life without the greenness of loving, and being loved. And now what she feels courses through her whole life, and makes it good.

Not that she's not going to change her life, but. This thing is a beginning, not an end. To confirm that, today she has booked two weeks leave that she was owed. They will have two weeks together, just her and Alastair. No worries.

Ahead of her Anne sees Julia come out of the Westpac place where she works. She watches her fat backside move up the Hill in her orange-cream dress. She thinks, Jeez, Julia used to be a real Latin beauty but now look at her. She's put on weight and she's spoiled her hair with a heavy perm and she plasters make-up on so she looks like a doll. Julia's really gone downhill since she started with Eddie.

Anne will go the other way with Alastair. She thinks of him and she sees Cambridge University, in images from *Brideshead Revisited* and *Chariots of Fire*: she sees ancient, echoing halls, and sunlight playing on a carved fountain in a leafy quad. She thinks of Alastair, and sees the civilized places she always dreamed of.

She wonders if she should rush to catch Julia up but then she thinks, not today. Today Anne walks slowly up the Hill, enjoying the sun on her face, watching Julia's fat backside sway ahead of her.

*

One night, a month later, they're lying in bed, she and Alastair, and she's looking at him, wanting to talk. He's lying on his back, smoking a cigarette, his big muscular chest rising and falling. She's looking at his soft brown eyes, blinking up at the ceiling, his long, feminine eyelashes.

She says, 'Al, can we talk?'

He says, 'Sounds like it.'

'No, I want to talk.'

'You are talking.'

Logical Alastair. His mind is made for games, crosswords, science, inquiry. He's always looking things up in his dictionary. He even looked up Parramatta: there's a kind of dress fabric named after it. After that he went through other clothes things named after places, denim, jodhpurs, balaclava helmets . . . Nick calls him 'Spock' sometimes. But she likes the way he seeks knowledge out.

She says, 'Al, what would you say if I said I thought I might be pregnant?'

Alastair blows smoke up into the air, like a whale spouting. He says, 'If, if, if. Hypothetical. What are you saying?'

She says nothing and his forehead furrows in the silence. He says, 'You're on the pill, aren't you?'

'I am now, sure. But when we started . . . I was real drunk . . . I can hardly even . . .'

He closes his eyes, draws air through his teeth, says nothing.

It's the face she saw the day they went to Bondi Beach. What happens is Alastair buys a car for him and Nick, an old white Toyota, for six hundred bucks. So on her first Monday off work, she and Alastair drive out to Bondi Beach together to test it out. They lie on the beach, reading and watching the surfers, and the sun doesn't seem too hot today and this is like real mellow. Only on the way back the Toyota starts stalling. When it stalls Alastair does the face: closed eyes, air through the teeth, ill-concealed rage.

A couple of times they flag people down and get going again with jump leads. But the car keeps stalling and finally Alastair goes apeshit. He gets out and starts kicking and punching the car like John Cleese in Fawlty Towers: he leaps onto the roof and starts jumping on it.

It's comical, he's not really serious in his rage, and yet

there's something about Alastair's car going down she doesn't like. She thinks of her old man in Broken Hill, repairing cars. He'd be bending over some kid's suss motor with the hood up and he'd shake his head and say, 'Your car's your life out here, mate.'

Maybe it's not so different in Parramatta. They have lived together, slept together for a month now, and it's, like, all right, but they're not going any place. She wants to talk, she says, but they don't talk. She asks Alastair about his plans, but Alastair says, 'My plan is to have no plan.' She wants to talk about, you know, the way they feel about each other, but he's not into that. She tries to talk and it's like turning the ignition key in an old car that won't start.

So what can you do? The night they get back from Bondi the guys all go to play snooker and she talks to Julia about it all. But Julia just goes on about Eddie, how he's too fat, too childish, too selfish. She complains about how he's influenced by Nick these days and how he uses Nick's stupid slang. Anne lightens up and talks about Alastair's snoring and the way he turns over in the night and his big arm lands on her like it would cut her in two. They talk about sex, and the way guys have a problem coming over with their emotions, you know, just talking. This is all right, it's good to be on a level with Julia again, the two girls with their two Pommie guys. But still she doesn't know what she can do.

So a couple of nights later she tries the pregnancy thing, thinking maybe this will get him talking. But all she gets is Alastair's stalled-car face.

And now he says, 'So what are you saying? You're saying you think you might be pregnant?'

She thinks and says, 'I'm not sure.'

'So you're not sure whether you think you might be? Bloody hell.'

He stubs the cigarette and turns away from her. She should be sore with him for reacting like that but she can't manage it. She says, 'Hey, I've been late before, don't worry about it,' and she starts to run her fingers down the groove of his hard, sculpted back. She should be sore with him but her fingers cross the ridges of his lateral muscle and explore his chest, and slide down his abdomen with its furrowed muscles running across, and down into the warmth of his groin, and she whispers: Hey. Don't worry about it. And when he turns and kisses her, and when he mounts her, and when she feels him inside her, then, oh God, oh Jesus, it's good, it's beautiful, it's all right now, it's okay now, she has no doubt.

But half an hour later he's snoring like a road drill and she's still lying there, awake, although it's nearly two in the morning, thinking about where they're going.

Her two weeks' leave pass real quick like this. Because of the late nights they don't get up til after midday. They watch TV: the car doesn't work so they can't go anywhere much. Alastair's a bit of a juicehead and every night he has to get drunk. If he's working, he comes in at midnight and then starts getting drunk. So it's another late night and he has no problems with the alcohol like they say, but afterwards he can sleep and she can't. And so it's another sleep in, until Monday comes a third time and she has to go back to work.

Now if she sits up half the night waiting for Alastair she gets hardly any sleep. But if she flakes out, she knows Nick will sit up with Alastair trying to talk him into leaving her. Nick's fed up with Parramatta, with his building job, with Eddie. He kips in the evening and then gets up later, and starts talking about Cairns. He says, 'Let's go to the Reef, Al. This is Hades, Al. Let's go to the Reef.' His mournful grey eyes fix on Alastair, try to take him from her. He's not gay, not according to Alastair, but the pair of them share their money like they were married, and if Alastair is to stay with her he'll have to, like, get a divorce.

What can she do? She takes this for a couple of weeks, but her eyelids are getting heavy and her stomach's all knotted up. So she gets another fortnight's leave by spinning the boss a yarn about her sick mother. At least she'll get some rest now.

So once more Monday is a long sleep against Alastair's back. She's feeling good when she gets up late to make the tea, and starts when she sees Nick, sitting there on the sofa with bandaged paws, reading an airmail letter that's come.

There's a bandage round his leg, too. She says, 'Jeez. So what happened to you?'

'Fell through a roof. Missed a strut and fell straight through.'

'So how long will you be off work?'

'A week, at least,' says Nick. 'Assuming I go back to work, that is.'

So Nick will be around the house now the whole time, trying to persuade Alastair to leave. She goes through to the kitchen to make the tea, trying not to be angry with him for falling through the roof, trying not to hate him. She stares through the hatch at him, her rival, sitting with his mournful grey eyes fixed down on the pale blue sheets of airmail paper. She watches as he removes two pages of the letter, and stuffs them into his pocket.

She wasn't spying on him, but the image stays with her. So what's so special about these pages? What's his secret? When Alastair gets up, he shows him the letter with the two leaves still missing. So Nick's told his Cambridge friend about her and Alastair, and . . .

She knows that's silly and arrogant, like thinking people in the next room you can't quite hear are talking about you. She knows that, but she can't help thinking it.

Anne doesn't get much to do except think, this day. Nick and Alastair are into chess at the moment and they play chess, game after game, for hours, Alastair winning mostly. Later they say they're going to the bottle store and when she asks if she should come Nick says, No thanks. She knows they have gone to the pub and they will stay there all evening. Anne sits on the sofa and sees them talking over their schooners of beer and Winfield cigarettes, talking about – what? She sees but she can't hear. She thinks again about Nick's secret pages.

Eddie and Julia come in, make a lot of noise, have showers, ignore her, go down the bowling alley. Anne sits watching the TV, alone, not caring what she watches. *The Perfect Match* is on and a middle-aged couple tells the smarmy host how they got on with their weekend in Surfers'. As ever they'll be back after this short break. Now the guys in khaki shorts from the Garden Centre are mowing the prices down. There's Rita the Eta eater with her simply beaut soft blend. The kids sing, Good on yer mum, Tip Top's the one, good on yer mum. Bearded toughs in a pub drink low alcohol beer and chant, Export Lite, mate, drink it all night, mate, it's all right, mate, it's all right: la-la-la-la, la-la-la-la, la-la-la-la . . .

Jeez. She tries to picture her life before Alastair came, and this is all she sees: an endless stream of advertising breaks viewed from the sofa. She kills the picture and goes through to her bedroom.

Anne lies on her big water bed, and turns and looks at herself in the dressing-table mirror. Her white nightshirt reads 'ailartsuA ni daM.' She looks thin and pale: she never gets out in the sun enough. Sometimes she looks good, sometimes her face is full of character, her skin is like ivory, she's all right. But right now she's just a pale girl with pallid, office-girl skin and mousy hair.

She and Alastair have lived together, slept together, for a month now. It should all be clear now, she should be able to see what will happen. But all she can see is this pale girl in the mirror who has fallen in love. Love to her has become like Nick's Reef: she cannot imagine life unless she can go there. She lived before, she got by, but then she knew nothing of the Reef. Now she must lose herself in the warm blue water, amongst the rainbow corals, amongst the glittering fish. She must lose herself again and again, with Alastair, for only he can take her there.

It's about midnight when she hears Alastair and Nick come in. She has the door ajar but with the light off. Nick speaks loud when he's drunk. She hears him say,

'No. This fugue must end.'

'Fugue?' Alastair goes for his dictionary. 'Fugue. One. Polyphonic composition in which short melodic theme – "subject"- is introduced by one part and successively taken up by others and developed by interweaving the parts?'

Nick says, 'Not exactly.'

'Fugue. Two. Loss of awareness of one's identity, often coupled with a disappearance from one's usual environment?'

Nick says, 'I am a Bach subject lost in a song by Kylie Minogue. Sod it, Al. Let's go.'

Alastair says, 'We can't.'

'Come on, Al. Let's exeunt. Depart. Vamoose. Say adieu. On y va. Hit the road. Take a powder. Change our names to Gough. Or failing that, let's just go, shall we?'

'We're pissed and we've got a car that doesn't work,' says logical Alastair. 'Besides which . . .'

He deliberately lowers his voice and now there is only muttering. She lies there awake a long time, not moving, like her limbs have gone numb. When at last there is silence she goes through in her dressing-gown. Alastair has fallen asleep on the sofa. She looks at him, sitting upright, his mouth open, smelling heavily of beer, wheezing in the way that means he'll be snoring soon: pathetic, she tells herself, he's pathetic. But she lies again in the big water bed and it is she who misses him, she who feels his absence as a great dumb ache.

She can't sleep, and once more she thinks of Nick's letter from Cambridge. The night is long and the square of her curtain is beginning to lighten, and still the letter torments her, like low voices talking about her in the next room.

She knows now what she must do.

Friday Nick limps back to work and Alastair's on his long shift, so at last she's alone in the flat. It's one in the afternoon and she has the curtains closed against the sun and the lunchtime news on the TV as she goes through Nick's bags, patiently, until she finds the sheets of crumpled airmail paper.

She reads.

Dear Nick,

how nice to hear your hyperborean tones once more. And yet, as you're aware, how not-completely-satisfactory is the telephone. So let me reflect more fully . . .

Sure, sure. She checks the pages: yep, the letter is all there, and two pages are more crumpled than the rest. She soon finds what she wants.

Your tales of Parramatta puzzle me. Whilst it is clear that you and Al both left us to seek 'something different,' I was not aware that this would entail swapping a wholly agreeable life for an entirely miserable one. Is it that your lives in the Antipodes are truly an inversion of our own? I note how Over There you seem to invest in cars that don't work; you send your weedy little guy out to dig ditches while the musclebound guy takes a bar job; you live with people you despise . . . I could go on. In fact, I will go on. What more evidence do I need for my hypothesis than Alastair's romantic

*activities 'down under'? Over Here in Cambridge, even as be-
nighted a couple as Diana and I find in lovemaking something to
lift our relationship above the truly abject. Yet Over There, for
Alastair, apparently, Alastair who must get roaring drunk ere he
can offer his affections to his hostess in her watery bed, sex is the
worst of it all . . .*

*If I understand the matter correctly, which I sincerely hope I
don't, Alastair sleeps with this girl in first instance because completely blotto and in farther instances in order to maintain your
minimal-rent accommodation. No. Surely not. Perhaps this pregnancy question offers a more logical explanation. When Alastair
said he was going to Australia to start a new life, were we in fact
meant to take this literally?*

Anne folds the leaves of the letter over and drops them back
into Nick's bag, and as she does so she sees again her image of
Cambridge University, with its ancient halls and leafy quads.
But now she hears laughter, raucous, male, locker-room
laughter, rising to a roar and echoing through the hallowed
corridors of Cambridge at this great Australian joke that Nick
has told his friends.

Then she goes apeshit. She goes through to the bedroom
and tears all the clothes off the bed and puts them in the gar-
bage chute. She gathers Alastair's clothes in a heap, and she
pours wine all over them, the cheap cask wine Alastair and
Nick drink, like it was petrol. And she gets a pair of clothing
scissors, and hunts out Alastair's favourite jeans, his favourite
shirt.

But the rage is passing, or turning into something else. She
can't take it out like Alastair takes it out on his car that stalls,
punching and kicking and roaring and jumping on the roof.
It's all inside. So she just sits there with his jeans over her lap
and the scissors in her hand, her eyes hot and dry, staring at the
dumb-show of the afternoon soap on the TV screen.

When Eddie and Nick come in just before five she's put all Alastair and Nick's things into a big pile in the middle of the lounge carpet. She's tidied up the rest of the flat so this big mound looks kind of weird. Anne thinks of Richard Dreyfuss in *Close Encounters*, when he builds the model of the hill in his house and his wife thinks he's nuts.

'Been tidying up, then?' says Eddie, grinning.

'I did an unforgiveable thing,' says Anne, and she hopes she sounds calm, in control. 'I went into Nick's bag and read his letter.'

It takes three trips for Eddie and Nick to get all the gear out and into the old Toyota in the car park. At last Eddie comes back alone, and tells her they've pushed the old car out onto the road. Nick and Alastair will sleep in it tonight, he says, and in the morning a new car will come, and they will drive away.

She just nods, sitting on the sofa with her arms folded. Eddie grins and says, 'Nice one, Cleo.'

She knows Cleo is the name of a dog at one house where Nick and Eddie were working. A real dumb dog.

Night is watching the figures change on the digital alarm clock, waiting for the curtain square to lighten. In the morning she hears an engine revving out on the road. She gets up real quick and goes up to the roof of Macquarie Towers.

Down on the road the old Toyota is nose to nose with another car, connected with jump leads, so far down they look like toys. Something must work because the hoods go down, the jump leads are packed away. There's Alastair, a toy soldier Alastair, shaking hands with a guy with a beard, who drives off in the Toyota. There's Nick, little Nick tiny from up here, and Nick and Alastair wave at the car, and then they hug each other, and they do a little dance, like a haka or something. Alastair takes the driving seat in the other car, a mustard-

coloured car, and Nick's elbow is out on the ledge of the passenger door as she hears the whine of the automatic transmis-
sion, and they're gone, away down Parramatta Hill, bound
for the Reef, toy figures in their dinky car.

They do a little dance. They do a little dance and drive away
in their little car. Her heart is full of bitterness and contempt.

Anne stands on the roof and looks at the shapes on the eastern horizon, the skyscrapers of the City. The dazzling white
morning sun rises behind them: the City looks like a fairy
place. In between and all around stretch the endless suburbs,
the endless houses, the endless roads. It makes her think of the
vast, roaring silence of the bush.

She goes back down to the flat. Eddie and Julia are making
love in their room, and the door isn't closed properly. They
sound like two boisterous kids on a trampoline.

Anne sits on the sofa and thinks of the day Alastair's car
works, and they go to Bondi Beach. She thinks of how she lies
on the beach and looks at the surfers out in the sea. Maybe it's
just coming from the bush, and maybe it's just she feels good
that day, but she loves this. She loves to see the guys balancing
on their boards, just before the big breakers turn white and the
ocean laps blue and white on the concrete-smooth sands.

Soon enough the guys fall off and go under. You wonder if
they'll hit their heads on the boards or get caught in the under-
tows but, sure enough, they emerge and pick up their boards
and go out again, and once more they balance, and once more
they fall, and once more emerge.

She thinks there must be something here, something to hold
onto, here, on the beach where she was happy, watching the
surfers.

Tasha Pym

Ice Cream

The choice of flavours was unusual for such a small kiosk.

'What shall we have?' she asked him.

He was looking at a group of people standing on the green in the middle distance.

'Karl?'

'What?'

'What d'you want?'

'Oh . . .um . . .' He pressed two fingers into his forehead and frowned at the array of tubbed colours before them. 'Anything,' he said. 'You choose.'

She watched him look over at the group again. The shadow of his cap fell low across his face and she followed its line over his nose and cheek, round to his earlobe.

Turning back to the kiosk she asked,

'What's the nicest?'

The ice cream girl stared out beyond them at the park, chewing on gum and gripping her scoop.

'They're all nice,' she said.

A man had arrived and was standing looking at the ice cream picture-board. His hands were stuffed deep in the pockets of his shorts, pulling the material taut across his buttocks.

'Karl, d'you like cherry?'

Distracted again, he looked at her, squinting.

'What? Yeah – fine – whatever.'

'Two cherries then, please,' she said to the ice cream girl, as Karl leant forward and touched her on the shoulder.

'I've got to see someone about something important,' he said. 'I'll be back in a minute.' And he ran across the grass, pulling his cap off and slapping it against his thigh, and disappeared down the bank out of sight.

The man blew out through puffed cheeks and jangled coins in his pocket, his bald head glistening in the sun.

The ice cream girl sighed and, looking at her now, said, 'Normal or wild?'

It was a hot day for September and, although it was late in the afternoon, the park was full of people. From where she was standing at the top of the bank, she could see right across the park to the lake, and beyond that, to the road. She watched Karl's black figure define the distance between them, leaving people strewn behind him like discarded garments as he ran. He was greeted by someone taller than himself, who came out from the group with one arm raised, ready to slap him between the shoulder blades in a gesture of brotherly welcome. For a moment they stood in conversation before joining the rest, who were standing huddled together in a pack except one who stood slightly apart, tossing spherical objects into the air above him.

She couldn't tell if she'd met any of them before. She was too far away.

Looking down at her hands, she clicked her tongue in her mouth. A smooth liquid gleam covered the tops of the ice creams and pink droplets nestled between the cones and her skin. She bit the inside of her lip and looked both ways along the bank. A dark strip of hair slid out from the clasp at the nape of her neck and dangled before an eye and down one cheek. Blowing it out like a streamer, she set off across the top towards the bandstand.

Within two hundred yards, the droplets had amassed to a precarious brim above her grip, which threatened, at any moment, to overflow down the backs of her hands, and she carried the cones quickly, like eggs on spoons, diagonally down the bank in the direction of some trees.

Two men came towards her, both overdressed for the hot afternoon in heavy dark trousers. One wore a sweater. They walked slowly and in unison, each with their hands clasped behind their backs, deep in discussion, and as their minds formulated opinions to exchange with one another, their eyes took in the melting spectacle which approached and passed behind them.

She stopped, rubbing her temple awkwardly against her bare shoulder in an effort to tuck the strand of hair behind her ear, and small rivers of ice cream scribbled their way down the layers of her fingers and clung along the crevices between each one.

'Bloody hell, Karl,' she whispered to the sagging mass in her hands, and the strip of hair danced on her breath.

It was cool under the yellowing trees, and the shadow they cast moved over the grass like water, lapping at the sunlit green. She was sitting cross-legged between the roots of a large oak, her elbows resting on her knees, the wet cones held out over the grass.

Two girls, who were lying sprawled on their fronts in the sun just beyond the branches, now and were looking over at her, nudging each other and laughing. Every few moments they would turn and look again across the green behind them, but seeing no one coming to claim an ice cream, began to pass comments to one another.

She ignored them and looked out across the green through a bunch of young boys who were playing football. She could pick out Karl easily now because, out of the group, he was only one of two left standing and talking still to his friend. The other six, including the juggler, were sitting in a commune on the ground.

The two girls began tussling, pulling at each other's

T-shirts and laughing, and she watched as the larger one straddled her partner, pinning her down by the wrists. The girl underneath tossed her head to and fro, her red hair shining as it caught the sun. The victor sat poised above, awaiting submission, then claimed her prize, bending her stubbled head to kiss her lover's neck and ear. Then, looking up abruptly, she grinned at the girl holding melted ice creams and released her partner, rising up on one knee and then standing. Her partner stood too, brushing grass from the backs of her legs, and they walked hand in hand through the shade towards the bandstand.

She watched them out of the corner of her eye as they began to nudge each other again, looking over at her, and once they had passed and were out of sight, she heard one of them shout, 'Don't forget to use a condom when he comes!' and the other one add, '*if* he comes, that is!'

The cones lay in her hands like soft cardboard cups filled with pink liquid, and her fingers ached from holding them. Adjusting her grip slightly, she waggled her fingers and breathed in deeply through her nose, enjoying the smell of wood and grass.

Wispy clouds flecked the blue sky and people had begun to drift out of the park, filtering onto the roads. The footballers had moved further towards the lake and the green between Karl and herself was clear. She saw him turn and look up the bank towards the kiosk. The ice cream girl was pulling down the metal shuttering, her figure silhouetted against the pale sky. He turned back to his friend and she imagined he might be saying, 'I'm gonna have to go now. I've got an ice cream waiting for me up there.' – and his friend would ask, 'Who you with?' – to which Karl might reply, 'That new girl.'

She watched his lanky friend issue another slap and raise his arm up above him as Karl turned and ran back the way he had come, his cap jutting up in the air. His friend watched for a moment, his arm still raised, then, letting it fall, he rejoined the group.

Karl's strides were long and he covered the ground quickly, his head held high and his chest arched out. Slowing to a walk, he pulled the cap from his head and stopped, shading his eyes with his forearm to scan the bank twice before catching sight of her under the trees.

She watched steadily as he ran towards her, slowing again to a walk as he came under the canopy of branches, panting and dropping his cap on the ground, his eyes searching her face, and as he reached her, he fell to his knees, took the soft cones from her and let them drop onto the grass, and taking her wet, pink hands in his, he kissed them and pressed them to his cheeks.

Archie Clifford

How can you lose something as big as a mother?

from *Quartet in a Flat*

Some people are gifted with memories that stretch back virtually to the cradle, and are able to recall countless childhood incidents with almost photographic clarity. I am not one of these people. My own memory is a fickle beast. It remembers what it wants, not what I would have it. That is why I have never been much good at examinations, or dates, or quotations, or remembering the great events of history. It has not been for the want of trying. Forgetting is the shears with which you cut away that which you cannot use, doing it under the supreme direction of memory, said Kierkegaard.

The earliest memory of any significance I *can* recall (despite myself, I might add, having spent the best part of thirty years striving to forget it) is of queuing in the playground outside the school dining-hall one spring day, at the age of eight. Even now if I close my eyes and think back, I can still remember it vividly: the noisy bedlam of fellow children at play all around me; the frantic footfalls of chase and pursuit, the screaming and the laughter; the wet smack of a leather caseball against a brick wall, the chink of the hopscotch stone as it landed; the rhythmic slap of a skipping rope; the insistent tinkle-clang of the teacher's bell summoning metallically from afar; and the celebratory squit squit squitting of a blackbird as it bombed in low under a bush near the perimeter railings; an invigorating mist hugging the damp tarmac at ankle-height as the climbing sun warmed the last puddles of winter and coaxed the sap into swelling buds, like the earth and everything in it was waking up from a deep slumber, coming alive; a sweetness in the air, like all the hopes of the future had been distilled to a thought which one could inhale. Then I thought, one day my parents are going to die.

They do say that April is the cruellest month.

*

Mothers. Who'd have one, eh? Don't they just screw our lives up from the very beginning? How? By giving them to us, for a start. I mean, did we *ask* for them?

I speak as a man of course, a son, which gives me a rather tenuous grip on the notion of motherhood, but I say it should be made compulsory for any woman contemplating childbirth to be in perfect health, have unsurpassed beauty, intelligence and wit, and the good fortune to be in possession of an enormous family inheritance . . . and much much more besides. Why? Because for the intended progeny, the absence of all these desirable attributes in the mother will invariably entail a lifetime spent in impoverishment and misery. Look at me, for instance. I was the last person she consulted before dragging me kicking and screaming into the world. If I'd had any say in the matter you can rest assured I'd have opted for birth into wealth and breeding, with all the happiness that invariably follows genuflecting in their train, rather than the drudgery and want which dogs their absence. Mothers, they just will not listen.

Take mine: a simple woman, submissive as opposed to obsequious, but polite to the point of painfulness. The phrase forever on her lips was 'Thank you very much, thank you very much.' As if she was in hock to the world for the rags on her back and the very air that she breathed. She would thank the government for raising inflation, the Social Security for reducing her allowance, the rent office for a fortnight's stay on the eviction order. Vulnerability emanated from my mother like the vibrations of a fly caught in a spider's web. The very Fates seemed to descend from their mountains, whole nations trek across continents to witness it, and to mock, this woman of almost Christlike meekness and humility. This loser. People would knock her down in the street and she would thank them for it. Football Pools companies would telephone her up to say that, yes, she *would* have won the jackpot, *if* the coupon had arrived on time. Did she complain? Bemoan her rotten luck? Of course not, not a bit of it; she thanked them for it instead, what else.

Then there were the doctors who used to queue up at the front door to tell her she had incurable diseases, on account of the fact that nowhere else would they have been received with such civility and gratitude, or offered in for tea and biscuits, and thanks. Many thanks. 'Thank you very much for telling me I'm going to die,' she would say.

I mean, politeness is okay up to a point, but taken to the extremes my mother did, well, it became a joke.

I'll be honest, mother could get on my tits sometimes. You probably guessed as much. Her ways irritated me. She was just too gullible, too ready to think the best of everyone. I didn't want her to be so meek and mild, so grateful for every little scrap and crumb that came her way. In short, I didn't want to inherit such martyrdom for myself. This is a vicious world we live in, a world of market forces and unbridled greed. If she wanted to let it crucify her along with all the rest of her class it was no business of mine, I thought; but when as a young child I began to notice some of her losing ways rubbing off on me, I decided it was time to act.

Mother needed training. She needed telling that in this life salvation is not to be found down the local bingo hall or in a buckshee pair of Premium Bonds.

Many was the time I was reduced to doing clandestine

favours for her in the dead of night, sneaking off in the vain hope that for just once in her life she would accept something without showering her benefactor with humble gratitude. And that by small but insensible degrees I could change her into the sort of selfish bastard of a taskmaster I knew was essential for my own future well-being. But no. There it would be five minutes later, her voice ringing exasperatingly in my ears: 'Oh, by the way, thank you very much for doing this or that for me.'

I wanted to scream sometimes, to take her by the shoulders and shake her, tell her not to be so fucking grateful for all the shit life was throwing at her. I didn't want to be nurtured so, retarded by her own suffocating love, warmth and humility.

'God bless you' was another saying of hers that really hacked me off. She always ended her letters to me with it. Those letters, the spelling was atrocious; just about the only line I could be confident of deciphering was the 'Thank you very much my son . . . God bless you.' at the end. God knows why she always signed off like that; she wasn't at all religious. No, that is not strictly true. I suppose it would be fair to say she had a vague notion of Christianity, of a God, a heaven and a hell (whatever *they* are). But she most definitely wasn't a churchgoer in the traditional sense. Never had been. Superstition was my mother's religion, *Old Moore's Almanac* her bible. She was into avoiding black cats, walking around ladders, keeping hammers and shoes off of tables, that sort of thing. What had *she* got to thank God for anyhow? He certainly hadn't blessed her with much, except an acute sense of her own inferiority.

My mother didn't understand that the people she most admired and looked up to in life hadn't earned their way. She would have been astonished, for instance, to learn that the aristocratic types generally despised people of such plebeian origins as her own. Even had she known, she would probably have adored them all the more for their lofty disdain. Thanked them, I don't doubt. The last of the diehard royalists was my mum, her cupboard a shrine of magazines and newspaper cuttings to Lady Di and Prince Phillip, to the Duke of This and Dutchess of That, and all the rest of those fine people. Final demands from the Electricity Board would line the mantlepiece like a row of Christmas cards and yet mother would rather see the lights go out before she'd default on her subscription to *Monarchy*, a monthly periodical which it was her proud boast to have procured every issue of since its launch several aeons ago. Witness the television programmes too: the thirty-second bites at the end of news bulletins, when His or Her Royalness would be captured patting some urchin on the head, or planting a tree, or vice versa. Dare we speak at such times? Of course not; it would have been an unpardonable solecism. Silence reigned in our household then. As it did for *Crossroads*, *Neighbours*, *Blockbusters* and *The Price Is Wrong*, and all rest of that escapist shit they put out so that poor bastards like my mother might not ponder too deeply on the grinding sterility of their own existences. Can you believe her, she really did think all that stuff was for real!

My mother's problem was that she hadn't got an ounce of common sense. I guess that was part of the reason why we were always in debt; she was hopeless with money. You need brains with money. The trick is to make it work for you, rather than the other way round. My mother never mastered it. Rather, it mastered her. Moreover, as is often the case with those who know the meaning of want themselves, she squandered what little she did have on others. She gave extravagantly to charities and institutions, was rarely seen without a badge for The Blind on her lapel, a sticker for Cancer Research on her purse. No sooner would Dad drop his paypacket into her hand on Friday than she would be up the shops buying us worthless little toys and sweeties, splashing out on fry-ups from the chippy, stocking up the biscuit tins, nipping up the pub to fill the old man's pop bottles with draught ale from the outdoor, so that by Monday morning she would be borrowing our pocket money back off us again. Apologising, thanking, scraping the marge off the sugar sarnies so that it might last out the week.

Poor sod, she was Stan Ogden in skirts was mother, a no-hoper, living from hand to mouth. As long as she had her forty Players Navy Cut for the weekend, two bob for the meter, and her *Monarchy* subscription, then the world was all right by Mom. I do believe it was Melyvn Bragg who once said that 'it is the poverty of ambition that is the real poverty of the working classes.' A statement so true it could only have emanated from someone who hailed from the streets himself. I like old Mel. 'Mel the Oracle' I call him. Seems like a good egg to me; knows his onions, if you know what I mean. All that said though Mel, with all the ambition and the best will in the world, there is the little matter of the money too. Mother spent the best part of her life worrying about money, on account of the fact that she'd never had any. It was probably that, as much as the cigarettes and bad diet, which pushed up her blood pressure and ruined her heart. Or broke it, I should say.

There was the way she looked too. This bothered me most when I was in early adolescence, when I used to visit my mates at their houses, but never invited them to mine. Many was the time I'd envy them their slim, tall, elegant mothers, with their pretty dresses and witty turns of phrase, immaculate beehive hairstyles and high heels; money still in their purses on Wednesdays, fresh nets in the windows once a week. Class acts, real class acts. With the sort of affected posh voices that normally had my own mother ill at ease, fumbling self-consciously over her own want of eloquence in polite company, as she did. Especially with the gums and all. I always imagined all my mates would have liked to fuck their mothers, because I certainly wanted to fuck most of them. In my imagination I *had*.

But *my* mother . . . well, somehow I just couldn't imagine them reciprocating the dubious favour.

The trouble was, mother wore her class like a suit of clothes. Or rather, it wore her. Poverty clung to her like the parasite it is, the tapeworm in the innards of hope, chewing on the last fragments of her dignity. Right down to her national health glasses, with their cheap square tortoiseshell frames and thick 'television set' lenses, which made her eyes look as if they were always changing channels. What with those and the fact that she hadn't got a tooth in her head. Those gums were a sight to see at mealtimes. Facial calisthenics it was called: chewing from the hairline down.

The Hilda Ogden headscarf and curlers didn't help much either, the old mac that sloped on her rounded shoulders, the shuffling gait and dragged feet, the frayed shopping bags hanging limply at her sides; the little black zip-up booties like ill-fitting, flat-bottomed boats; the baggy face and downcast looks; the way the jumble sale dresses used to ride up over her fat knees, and those outdated silk blouse things she used to wear, struggling to hold in her ample sagging tits, filling me with embarrassment whenever I had to sit next to her on the bus. 'Why can't my mother look like yours?' I would think, 'or yours? or yours? or yours? – anything but like mine!' And 'why don't you slim?' I wanted to shout at her. And 'why don't you do something with your hair?' I did shout. 'I'm sorry,' her eyes would reply to my withering looks, 'if I don't come up to your expectations. I'm sorry if I'm not everything you wanted a mother to be.'

Bah! Let's not mince words any longer. Let's not indulge in euphemisms like 'a disarming innocence' or 'an endearing naivety'. Mother was thick. Mother was common. Mother was ugly. Mother and beauty had long since argued and fallen out. Mother and money, mother and intelligence, mother and the Twentieth Century, they just didn't get on. Do you know,

I actually caught her once, trying to melt cheese on her toast – *vertically? In the electric toaster?* 'It keeps falling off,' she said, with that lost, helpless, flustered, embarrassed look on her face, as I snatched the things off her and put them under the grill. (Yes, my mother's inadequacies could be summed up by a litany of such adjectives.) But when I shouted at her and told her how stupid she was, what do you think her reaction was? You guessed it: 'Thank you very much,' she said. 'God bless you for shouting at me son. I'm sorry. I'm sorry for being so ugly and stupid and worthless as a mother.'

'I'm sorry' – now there's another phrase I could talk about.

She was forgetful too, and clumsy: always spilling things down herself. She never did get the hang of eating without a bib, not since the teeth went west. And I never knew a woman who fell over and grazed her knees so much. If there was one raised flagstone in a thousand on the pavement, you could bet your last farthing on my mother finding it out with her toe. 'Thank you very much,' she would say to whoever was around to pick her up (and probably to the flagstone too, for breaking the fall of her chin). 'I'm sorry if I embarrassed you. I know I'm clumsy and stupid and ugly, Andrew. I didn't mean it,' she would say, as I stood around whistling and tapping my foot, trying to make out I didn't know this demented old fool of a woman scrabbling on her hands and knees in front of me.

There are a thousand similar anecdotes I could relate in testimony to my mother's unworthiness for matriarchy. But time and space demand brevity, so I shall summarize: too uneducated to realise the value of education for her own progeny; seemingly addicted to cigarettes, indigence and debt ever since she came into the world; plain rather than grotesque; too small, obese, and with the wrong colour hair and eyes (both black); the teeth of a jellyfish; riddled with heart disease, eczema, varicose veins and rheumatism. Just about the only thing she had, which a son might want, was a moustache. Who the hell would want to inherit the characteristics of a mother like that, eh? A masochist? An idiot?

What is it with this procreation thing anyhow? this bestowing of life? Who *asked* for it? What's the big deal? the angle? the point?

*

'*Life*,' said Hobbes, '*is solitary, poor, nasty, brutish and short . . . a war of every man against every man.*'

I think Hobbes has a point here. Hobbes could well be my man. Maybe they had a Tory government in his day too. I mean, look around you; what do you see? Every hour of every day a million insects fighting tooth and claw; birds, animals, people, tearing each other limb from limb. Even as I write a thousand beasts are devouring each other alive in some appalling Schopenhaurian nightmare. The stench of war, barely cleared from the skies above Kuwait, returns to pall the fields of Eastern Europe yet another year; a hundred thousand mutilated corpses bloat and shimmer with the jewellery of maggots under Iraqui sands; Kurds still freeze upon the mountain tops; millions starve and thirst to death in Africa; the kids root among the rubbish heaps in Mexico City and Rio; Serb shoots Croat, Croat Serb, Hindu Muslim, Tamil Sikh; a street implodes in Belfast, a blameless taxi-driver slumps dead over the wheel of his car, his grieving family over the remains of their shattered days; in the foul confines of some deep subterranean cell an electrode is applied to bruised genitalia; a cigarette sizzles on flinching skin; eyes are gouged, knees drilled, backs flayed . . . and all of this is happening now as I write, daily as we live and breath and eat. And all for what reason? All in the name of life? *Ha!*

If this is the best of all possible worlds, then for God's sake spare us the worst, I say.

Why did you bring me here mother? I was okay where I was. I never had a worry in the world until you brought me into it.

Look, we are born, life is a shit to us, and then we die. That's it. That's all there is. For the majority – those of us whose unfortunate destiny it is to have to serve out the full term of our natural lives – the normal sentence is sixty to seventy years. Bowed before the god called Mammon, up to our necks in debt, incarcerated high in the sky in office blocks or deep underground in mineshafts, factories, laboratories. If we're lucky money may come along to amuse us for a while, or AIDS to speed up the process of our despatch. But that is the most that we can hope for. Life is teleologically meaningless. It goes nowhere. We are dying from the moment we are born. All that exists just struggles towards an inevitable collapse into nothingness. Even the universe. A nothingness which, absurdly, we fear more than anything on this earth. Absurd, because what we are frightened of is the absence of all this drudgery and pain, this repression and violence, this bereavement over loved ones and fear of our own mortality. Absurd, because to crave immortality is to wish to cling to such a miserable existence as if we were enjoying the bloody thing. Whereas death contains nothing. Death is the absence of all that shit. Why fight it, I say.

No, mothers have just got things back to front, that's all. Diseases and illnesses have got the right idea. They know what to do with life. Get shut of it. There's just no contest; death wins hands down every time. Death's a doddle; it's a ball; you should try it some day.

*

'To be afraid of death is only another form of thinking one is wise when one is not,' said Socrates; 'of thinking one knows what one really doesn't.'

Quite. Exactly what I have been saying – death might be the greatest happiness that ever befell a man. Let me explain.

Death, for certain, is one of two things: either it is annihilation, and the dead have no consciousness of anything, or else it is the migration of the soul to another place. If the former, and there is no consciousness but only a dreamless sleep, death must be a doddle – one long endless peaceful night. If, on the other hand, death is a removal from here to some other place, where all our dear departed ones are, then what's so dreadful about that? I believe we are under a grave misapprehension to behold the prospect of this plunge into nothingness as some sort of evil. Indeed, I often think it strange that human beings should be so terrified of the millions of years they will not live to see, when the millions of years that existed *before* their birth appear to cause them no anxiety at all. Perhaps one could understand a little better their reluctance to depart, were it that life for most of them had been all sweetness and light. But for most it has not, yet even the lowest cur of a dog still clings on to the dregs of his bondage, as if it would be the most terrible catastrophe to be set free. Such fears are futile. Life is in vain; as is, therefore, the quest for immortality, which not even the universe possesses it in its present form, nor stars, sun, or planet. How preposterous then that such an insignificant little creature as *homo erectus* should wish to possess it. And where should he live if he did? When the universe was no more?

Far better then, on mature consideration, to have not been born or lived at all; to be absolved of all this pointless chattering and wringing of hands in what is after all only one microscopic corner of a meaningless and callous cosmos. Far better, instead of having the horizon of infinity stretching out on only one side of his existence, after death, for the individual to have it on both sides, for his absence to be surrounded in perfect symmetry by a beautiful, timeless, immeasurable void. Instead of the anxiety of 'being' there will be only the imperturbable unconsciousness of 'not being'. Or potential. Or 'might-have-being', one might almost say. Which is nothing, because all things might have been, but were not. A much better state of affairs for everyone concerned, don't you think?

It's no good, I've decided: it shall be decreed henceforth that all poor, ugly, ailing mothers will be forbidden to bear children. In Ethiopa, in South America, in China and in Wolverhampton, all the potentially impoverished, sick and needy of the world will not exist. I can't see that anyone will weep for them. I certainly won't. Will you? And as for they themselves, well, they will merely continue sleeping the blissfully unaware, eternal sleep of the unborn.

Or at least, this is what I used to think.

*

The second stroke came three years after the first; the third one three months after the second; the final one three weeks after the third. One has to marvel sometimes at this wonderful geometry we find in nature.

She didn't even realise she'd had the first at first. Slight numbness down the one side, temporary slurring of the voice, that was all. It wasn't even considered necessary I should break off my first year's studies to go home and visit her. She wouldn't hear of such a thing. And, selfish bastard that I am, I didn't need much persuading either. I was hot on the trail of some unsuspecting young geography fresher at the time, as I remember. With a prayer and a pocketful of condoms.

It had been a warning of course, for us all. We were nicer to her for a while, much nicer. Things always seem more valuable when you're in imminent danger of losing them. I sent her cards and things; you know, the ones with all that sentimental poetry crap on the front – about how she and Dad were the best parents a kid could hope for. Stuff about mountains and rainbows, the wind and the rain, ying and yang, ding dong, let's all walk off into the sunset together holding hands. Yeah, like I said, we were much nicer to her for a while. Then of course she seemed to get better, and we started to take her for granted again.

It wasn't until a year or two later that I realised she'd never really gotten over the initial stroke. Not properly. I remember, it was during the weekend she came down to Brighton for the graduation ceremony. There I was, all dressed up in my gown and mortarboard, liberally anaesthetized with a quarter bottle of Teachers, feeling the part. It was a nice sunny day so we decided to walk to the Brighton Centre along the seafront. By the time we'd got half way along however, mother suddenly got out of breath and had to sit down. It was only the lightest of breezes in our faces, but we had to flag down a taxi in order to continue. That shocked me that did. I never realised things were that bad.

The second stroke was much worse though, a hospitalization job, so I had to rush up from Brighton to Wolverhampton to see her. I had long since graduated by then of course, so I was glad of the chance to get away for a few days. I stayed a week, that was all. I never told her I was coming. It was supposed to be a surprise. (For her, not me.) Oh God! what a depressing experience it turned out to be, visiting her in that ward of ailing bodies, where none looked more shrunken and feeble than hers. Where was she, I thought, as I made my way over towards the ghost of a woman lying on the corner bed.

'Hello love! Here he is! I told you he'd come! This is my son, my Andy.'

I never saw such pride and joy on those ravaged features as when she laboured across the tiles to embrace me. It was as if I'd been away a whole lifetime. 'God bless you for coming son,' she cried. 'Oh, thank you very much for coming. I . . . I'm sorry if I've been a trouble to you, if it's been a nuisance coming up all this way just to see me. I'm sorry I've been ill.'

Was that *her*, I thought, incredulous at the extent of her demise. Reduced to *that*? So breathless, just sitting up in bed or walking the few paces across the floor. What had happened to that vibrant energetic woman I had known all my life? That woman who had washed and scrubbed and worked and cooked and borne and raised and carried and fetched? This wasn't my Mom, this wheezing frail old woman whose cheeks had suddenly pinched overnight, whose limbs had shrunk, shuffling around in those borrowed fluffy pink slippers and dressing gown.

Ah yes, death was ganging up on her for sure, and I was powerless to stop it.

Most of the others in the Cardiac Ward looked younger than mother, even though she was only sixty four. She had aged ten years in as many months. Her body was ailing, moribund, whereas theirs looked more resilient, their demeanours cheerful, their prognoses confident of recuperation. In mother's eyes I read only fear, abandonment, yearning. Yet still she clung on to life like it was something beautiful. Because she didn't want to die. Because she was ignorant and fearful of what it meant to die. If only I'd had the courage to tell her what a doddle it was; and how much pleasanter death would be than the melancholy shadow of her ailing life; how sweet and painless would be the long night of sleep that lay ahead of her. If only . . . if only . . . if only I too hadn't wanted her to die.

It should have been a time for intimacy, of course, and would have been, had we but known. But in the crowded confines of that bustling ward privacy had no dominion. What little we snatched we squandered in our usual way, with me insisting I should come back home if she really wanted it, she insisting she wouldn't hear of such a thing . . . and both of us knowing we were telling lies.

I took her in a different jigsaw every day; a few boiled mints and diet drinks. But the cigarettes and chocolates – the small sweeteners that had made life tolerable in the past – were to be denied her now. It was imperative, the doctors said, that *however* long she had left to live, she was to be made as miserable as possible for the entire duration. Not in so many words of course, but it amounted to the same thing, to mother. She never had been one for all that vegetarian healthfood stuff: watercress, spinach, cutlet of nuts. Bacon sandwiches, pig's trotters, black pudding and tripe, fried bread, liver and onions – I tried to tell the doctors what she really liked. But they knew best, so they said.

Well, a fat lot of good *they* did her didn't they, with all their roughage and cholesterol-free advice. If I'd known then what I do now I'd probably have snook her in a few Quality Street, let her smoke herself silly those last few months. Who knows, she might even have been with us now if we'd let her. She'd certainly have been a lot happier. I reckon unhappiness kills a person quicker than anything. Besides, what's the point of living if everything that brings us enjoyment is prohibited? To listen to some doctors you'd think that everything we ate and drank was bad for us, that if we stopped eating and drinking altogether we'd probably live for ever and ever. And I never did hear two doctors who agreed about what *was* good for us.

I don't know, sometimes I really do wonder about the wisdom and efficacy of the medical profession. Maybe it's time we considered putting a government health warning on some of these quacks:

> ## WARNING: DOCTORS CAN SERIOUSLY
> ## DAMAGE YOUR HEALTH
> ## SEEING DOCTORS CAN TAKE YEARS
> ## OFF YOUR LIFE.

A fag a day keeps the doctor away, that's what my old Mom used to say. Yeah, I think I might take up the habit myself soon, just to spite the bastards. It's a bit late in life I admit, mid-thirties, but I'm a quick learner.

*

A fine dutiful son I am, I don't think. I couldn't even wait the extra day until she came out of hospital. Brighton was calling again you see. I was itching to get back to my desk, to the writing, my world of fiction. To leave reality, mother, behind. All too readily I agreed with her selfless decision that, should she suffer a third or subsequent strokes, requiring further hospitalization in the near future, it would be pointless for me to keep trapsing back home all the time. I had my own life to live after all, she said. I couldn't just drop everything and keep legging it half way across the country every time her heart had a little flutter, now could I?

It was a time for goodbyes. To the detached observer she would probably have cut a rather pathetic figure. The outsize dressing gown had fallen open. Her sad, deflated, caved-in breasts were scarcely evident under the faded nightie as her chest rose and fell with sobs. She stood trembling at the hospital window, waving me goodbye as she so often had from the doorstep at home; watching me all the way to the corner and out of sight. I could hardly bring myself to look back. My eyes filled up as I wondered whether I would ever see her again. True, I had felt like this on countless previous occasions, and had taken comfort from the fact that she had always been there when I returned, but in my heart of hearts I knew that one day, sooner or later, she would not be.

Would that I had known the truth, of course, and wild horses wouldn't have dragged me away from her that day. But we are not to know, are we. Not the truth. How else could life play its little jokes on us.

The lips were puckered, the eyes screwed up, the tears streaming down her sunken cheeks. Her hair was still thick, but coarser and greyer now, and several small clusters of it stood in high relief on the moles that dotted her forehead and chin. Pupils had faded, glazed over with the pinks and browns of the body's inner corruption. Time's wrinkles deepened as her bushy eyebrows knitted in a rhythmic lament, furrowing together above a snivelling bulbous nose. The skin's pallor was grey, translucent, ghostly. I don't think I ever beheld a more beautiful sight than my mother's weeping face, the last time I ever saw her alive.

C. M. Rafferty

Mary Cleary ate my Orange

Leonard Chimney wrote erotic poetry in aid of Nicaragua and did a bit of cookery on the side. He walked around the basement in his Harem pants, an orange under his armpit, and from time to time was struck by something particular in his book.

'Too true' he'd say and make a note of it by the light of the electric fire.

He put the book down and chose a table fork from the floor, lifting it with both hands in swoons towards the ceiling and inserting it into the orange with small, formal gasps.

He put on his glasses and examined the moon through the window, constructed a compass from the fork and a feather and double-checked the angle of Venus. He dipped the feather in invisible ink and pondered the instructions while chewing his lip. The shadow of the moon was dip-dipping by the window pane and he took the orange out and drew a circle on it from top to bottom, then he tucked it back under his armpit and lay on the bed, which was a tabogan.

Under the plush green parallel bars of the reading lamps he had watched her pass, flicking her thumb through a list. Ve-ron-ica, the shining heels of her patent shoes reflecting his books and the wood. Behind the issue desk she cocked her head,

'Is that Chimney with an e?' she said.

Pure love.

He had tracked her through the audiovisual stands, bibliographies, cartomancy, demography, eudemonism, fructification, all those glittering tomes. Ve-ron-ica, never off his lips. Around the volumes of philosophy and plants, over her desk and her sandwich, pâté de fois gras she'd say, I never eat anything else.

He spent the days, those heady days, stalking the pony-tail out on the street, waiting in bushes while she shook her umbrella and tightened the loops on her belt. He followed her from the stop for the number twenty nine, down over the bridge, three roundabouts and a tobacco shop, down a footpath, up a hill and to a blue door with a brass plate and a hard cold concrete step where he sighed as she vanished within.

Veronica Sweetnam climbed the stairs and threw exhausted shoes across the room. So tiring, so on-her-feet, so pressurised, yet so rewarding, the people she'd meet. Mary Cleary listened in awe and staggered under plates of spiced stew, have a cracker Veronica, have a biscuit, have a bath and I'll make you hot soup.

Leonard Chimney whistled along from strength to strength. He followed her through some sneezing fits, two electricity strikes and an almost potentially serious bout of flu. She would swallow the pulp of her orange,

'Vitamin C Mr Chimney you understand, now what can I do for you?'

But today, disaster. At twenty nine minutes past noon, in the neat waxed aisle near the issue desk, Veronica Sweetnam tripped on his shoe and scowled as he seeped his apology. He pulled up the hood of his anorak in consternation and tried to continue with his reading.

Tonight he would bear her his gift.

Mary Cleary had done the dishes sixteen days in a row and she crossed her legs on the high back chair and said she would not be doing them again. And that was that. Except that she wouldn't be doing any shopping. Either.

Veronica Sweetnam shrugged her shoulders and turned the radio up. Mary would not be accompanying her to the cinema? And that was fine. Mary Cleary watched the pony-tail vanish down the stairs and tugged at the ends of her blouse in frustration.

Leonard Chimney stole to the kitchen and borrowed a bag of liver from his mother's fridge. He looked right and left on his tiptoes and closed the door without a squeak. He straightened his glasses and went to the window where he laid out the liver and hummed. Flicking through the book momentarily, he memorised the instructions, moved the orange from one armpit to the other and tapped his pale chest with his hands. He piped fifteen and a half minutes of incantations, and hopped the orange up and down the liver while examining the diagram again. He blew a round kiss through the window and smiled at the fruit of his love.

Pulling out the electric fire he connected the plug of a mushroom shaped lamp and wrote three verses and two instructions on a page of blue Belvedere Bond. He left his glasses in the sink, strapped back his pants with four bicycle clips and slipped his arms through his anorak. He wrapped the poem around the orange, raising his thumbs in salute, and folded it carefully into the zip-up pocket near his heart. He bundled the liver back into the fridge and went out the back way, whistling. Projecting himself at a distance from his bicycle seat he followed the path of the river, his clothes wafting semaphore over the bars.

It was, of course, a starry night.

Mary Cleary washed down the walls and steeped all the curtains in bleach. She bunched up her skirt in the palm of her hand and set off on all fours around the floor with a cloth and a bottle of liquid soap that gave off, she fancied, an odour of turnips and milk. She tested the route with the ball of her foot and, pronouncing it safe for a crossing, collected her coat from the back of a stool and decided to get some air.

Under the clock near the wooden bridge Veronica Sweetnam brushed cheeks with some friends and decided they had enjoyed the advertisements more. They swerved to the right to avoid a bike and decided to go back for tea. To the right of the door she flicked a switch and, wiping her shoes on the mat, dislodged a sheet of blue paper. Her name stretched in a spider across the flap and pausing to open it, she discovered a poem with instructions. She beckoned her friends up to the landing, reading as she went. At the top of the stairs they turned around and took three steps at a time to the bottom where they hummed and hawed and bundled around but couldn't locate any fruit.

Mary Cleary sat on a chair, the orange peel strewn at her feet. She squeezed the last pip through the grip of her molars and turned at the creak of the door. Veronica Sweetnam reddened to beet and, tossing the page with a pout towards the peel, said: 'Oh yes. And what am I supposed to tell Leonard Chimney?'

Patricia Debney

Dry Land

Patricia D

Marge stood in the kitchen stirring spaghetti. Only a year after they'd first seen the house and here they were. She could hardly believe it – Fred finally retired, the old house sold, the drive down from Virginia to Florida in a U-Haul, this house – for once, everything had worked out.

Now it was already two days after Christmas. She tried not to think about the turkey carcass in the refrigerator, but thought about it anyway. It needed finishing, but tonight she couldn't face it, tearing it apart, thinking about Christmas. Her sister Jean and her family, who lived nearby in Cape Coral, had come over Christmas Day for a big meal, ended up leaving too early. 'Everyone's tired,' Jean'd said, squeezing Marge's arm at the door, 'what with the new baby – but it was lovely, thank you.' Jean's youngest daughter had just had a son, her first, and everyone was a little nervous.

Marge nodded and crinkled up her eyes in return, shrugged her shoulders. 'Of course we understand.' But she'd gone to a lot of trouble, their first Christmas in the new house. It was depressing, and she and Fred had stayed up late watching old movies.

So tonight, she thought, to heck with it, they were having spaghetti. She imagined Fred in the next room dozing in his armchair. Since retirement he seemed to sleep a lot, and watch a lot of sports on TV.

Marge looked at her watch and threw the spaghetti in the water. When it was done she carried two plates through to the TV room, nudging Fred's leg on the way through. 'Hey you,' she said, 'dinner. Now be quiet, it's time for my programme.'

He started awake. 'Not that.'

'Yes that. Now shush.' She sat down carefully.

The handsome announcer came on. Organ music swelled in the background. 'Welcome to *Reunion*,' he began, and the camera followed him over to a light blue armchair in a soft focus TV living room. He sat down, and spread his hands out generously. 'You know,' he went on, 'tonight might be the first night of the rest of your life . . .'

'Looks like he got his teeth capped over Christmas,' whispered Marge.

'And the chairs re-covered,' said Fred, 'even homier.'

'So they are.' She sat on the edge of her seat, her plate balanced on her knees. Every time she took a bite, she brought the plate closer to her face by going on tiptoe.

The announcer was in full swing. 'Let's start tonight by looking at some success stories, more happy people brought together by *Reunion*.' There was a flash to two women, one older, one younger, both with permed hair and prominent noses, running full speed at each other in the arrival lounge of an airport. Their bodies collided and they started weeping uncontrollably. Mascara ran down their faces and gathered in the wrinkles around their mouths.

'. . . like Ann and Samantha Bristow, in Kansas City. When she was still a tiny baby, Ann was put up for adoption by her parents, who were too poor to look after her.' – 'How awful,' Marge interjected – 'Her sister Samantha didn't even know Ann existed until her parents passed away recently. Then she felt the need to get in touch with the only sister she had in the world. So she contacted us,' the picture switched back to the announcer pointing at his chest, 'and we contacted you, viewers,' he pointed at the camera, 'to find Ann. And as you can see, both are overjoyed at their reunion.'

There was a commercial break. Marge held her plate up and wriggled back in her chair, still staring at the TV. 'Shame the parents never knew the sisters met.'

Fred sighed noisily. 'Marge, you're too gullible. They say the same thing every week. It's manufactured.'

Marge shrugged her shoulders. 'I don't know, I just think it's heartwarming. Such a good feeling, that's what I think about . . .'

The announcer came back with another success story, about wartime lovers. Marge reached for a Kleenex. 'Honestly,' Fred said.

'Look,' Marge waved her tissue at the TV, 'even he's got a tear in his eye.'

'Glycerine,' said Fred.

Just then the announcer took out his handkerchief and dabbed his eyes.

'Honestly,' Fred said again.

'Now, as a break from all that,' the announcer croaked, smiling, 'let's look at some photo-searches.'

'Oh, good,' said Marge.

'Oh, dear,' said Fred, 'where's your plate?' He got up and carried their plates through to the kitchen.

Lively background organ music, like the kind used for early morning television fashion shows, accompanied the photographs that flashed across the screen.

'Robert Carey,' the announcer said behind a picture of a dark-headed, dark-eyed boy. 'This picture was taken twenty years ago by your great grandmother, who passed it onto her grand-niece, who's never met you. Robert, if you're watching – get in touch. This could be your Reunion!'

Fred swore in the kitchen, and there was the sound of silverware clattering to the floor.

Marge jumped up, sidled over to the doorway. 'You okay?' she called, still watching the TV. A picture of a little girl with blonde hair came on; she looked familiar.

'It's my knee,' he yelled back, then hobbled into the room.

'Thanks for your sympathy. Bang my knee and you watch TV. Great.'

'Ssshhh,' Marge grabbed his arm, 'look at this. Does that look like me?'

Fred looked up, eye level with the TV. 'If you mean aside from the fact that you're about fifty years older, no, I don't think so. You're imagining things.'

'I'm serious, Fred. I think he said "Marge Anderson."'

They listened to the announcer. 'Marge Anderson, if you're out there . . .'

'See! Oh my God, is it me?' She went up to the TV and stared at it.

'Marge, I can't tell -' he looked around, then picked up the instamatic from the coffee table and poked her with it. 'Why don't you just take a picture.'

'What?'

'So we can get a closer look or something,' he said, 'we need to use up the film anyway. Besides, I'll never hear the end of it.'

'Okay.' She took two, from different angles, to be on the safe side.

The show ended. Marge collapsed into her armchair. A toothpaste commercial came on, and Fred turned down the sound. 'Try not to get your hopes up,' he said, 'I'm not too sure. There must be a lot of Marge Andersons.'

'I know,' she said, 'but it would be nice, wouldn't it?'

'Yes,' he said, 'it would.'

Next morning Marge got up early to turn the film in. Jean and her family hadn't even stayed long enough to use up most of a roll, so Marge finished it by getting a picture of the breakfast table, then parts of the house; it looked good from the outside.

As she approached the drugstore she caught sight of herself reflected in the automatic doors. The sky behind her was light grey, and she couldn't help but see herself get closer and closer. I need a trim, she thought, reaching up to pat her white hair, looks like I've got horns. Her red windbreaker was too tight, the wrong size, reaching only as far as her waist, and her navy trousers swelled out from there. She couldn't resist, and stopped in the middle of the sidewalk, turned sideways to look at her stomach. Still Christmas dinner. Soon it would start spreading itself onto her hips, as usual.

Never mind, she thought. The doors swung open.

She waited a while in line, only to find when she reached the front that it was the wrong one. The woman behind the counter pointed to the next counter, which did, Marge noted, have a large Kodak sign above it advertising various Christmas family shots.

She smiled at the boy standing there and handed the film over. He made note of her name, 'Anderson,' on the envelope.

'Tomorrow afternoon,' he said, looking past her .

'Oh.' Marge was disappointed. 'Can't I . . .' she saw the Kodak banner out of the corner of her eye. 'Can't I pick it up, well, sooner? They're Christmas pictures, and you know . . .' The boy looked at her blankly, but said, 'Okay, five o'clock today, but that'll be another two dollars.'

'Fine,' she said, 'thank you.' She was so grateful she found herself almost dropping a sort of curtsy as she turned to leave.

When she got home, Fred was gardening as usual. Since the retirement he gardened every day, rain or shine. Today was flat and dull, the same as yesterday. Last year, when they first decided to move here, the sun was shining, in the middle of winter, and had kept on shining for days. They'd stayed at Jean's house.

Marge stood at the sliding glass doors a minute and watched Fred move slowly around one end of the lawn, pulling up crabgrass. Then she got her fishing cap – they'd been given matching khaki ones by her niece for Christmas – and went outside.

Fred stood up and waved. She waved back and made an 'okay' sign to let him know the film was in. He bent back down and she went over to the tiny palm tree they'd planted just after they moved in. Everyone in Florida had at least one palm tree in their garden, and she and Fred had decided to start from scratch so they could see it grow. But it hadn't been looking well recently, yellowed around the edges, leaves drooping. She craned her head back to look at the sky. Not enough sunshine, she decided, and reached out to touch it.

'Marge!' Fred had looked up at just that moment, and Marge stopped mid-reach. They were frozen there a minute, him looking at her across the lawn, her looking at the tree, her hand almost touching it.

She turned her head to look at him. 'What?' she said, bringing her hand back to tuck some hair under her cap, 'what?'

Fred came over to her. 'The tag says not to touch it very much, remember.' He looked at her pointedly.

'Yes.' She paused. 'But I wish you wouldn't call her an "it" - she's Delilah.'

'Well, Delilah then.'

'That's better. You know things grow better when they have a name.'

He rolled his eyes and rocked a little on his heels. 'That's what you say . . .'

'It's not just what *I* say,' she interrupted, 'Brian on Garden Talk says that too – he's *proved* it, actually!' She crossed her arms and looked up at her husband.

'Oh, well then, Brian is the expert, after all . . .' He trailed off, and they were silent. Then, as if on cue, they both pushed back their caps; Fred scratched his hairline and Marge brushed the horns out of her face. They surveyed the garden.

Fred especially had been working hard on the garden and it

was impossible to really know until spring if all the effort was paying off. Some basic landscaping had come with the house – grass planted, borders made. Round patches filled in with large Florida stones the size of melons, ready for palm trees, were spread around the yard like bald spots.

Fred shrugged. After the hills of Virginia, their garden here seemed disturbingly flat; Delilah was the first thing of any height they'd planted, and she looked frail, staked up in the middle of a pile of grey stones.

'Whatever does the trick,' he said, turning to Marge.

'Yes,' she said.

'That's what I think,' he finished, and walked back to one end of the lawn.

Marge bent back down over the palm tree. 'Delilah Mae,' she said, lightly brushing the leaves with her fingertips. She didn't know what else to say, but now that she was down here she felt she should make the most of it. 'Grow,' she said, 'come on, grow!'

By lunchtime the air and sky were oppressive. Marge had no idea it could be so muggy even in the winter. She stood at the kitchen sink mixing sweet corn into her tuna. Out the window she could see Fred's hat bobbing up and down irregularly.

'Fred!' She knocked on the window. The hat stopped for a moment, then continued. 'Fred!' She knocked harder and this time his face popped up, eyes squinting, eyebrows drawn in. 'Lunch!' she mouthed, holding up the bowl.

His face lit up and he gave her a thumbs-up sign.

Marge carried the bowl, some bread, and plates through to what they called the dining room. The house was designed for it to be the dining room, but in truth it was just a big room with a smallish table and two chairs around it. No glass cabinet, no sideboard, no family silver.

She tried not to, but she sometimes thought about it, about

how typical it was. Last year when they first saw the house, they didn't stop to think. They went ahead and spent everything they had on it, only to find when they arrived that it was just enormous, far too big for them. They didn't have enough furniture, or enough money left over to buy more. So the old living room suite was split up – two chairs in the TV room, the sofa in the living room – and the extra dining room chairs were distributed mostly in spare bedrooms. Only one spare room even had a bed; the others became half-flown sitting rooms, sporting lamps without tables, books without shelves, etc. At first, Fred despaired. *But think of the space!* Marge had said then, twirling around to the best of her abilities, arms open.

Now if she could help it, Marge only looked at the parts of the house that were full – their bedroom, the kitchen, to an extent the TV room. She didn't regret buying the house; it was ranch style, sprawling, a challenge for them, and she loved the paintwork – a grey-green and brown, the shade exactly between the grass and the winter sky – a welcome change from two-storey white clapboard. But the half-deserted feeling of it had never completely settled. After comforting Fred, she thought, what was there but a feeling of shrivelling up? She felt like if somebody came along one day and picked up the house and shook it, they'd just sound like two old berries rattling around. Not that it was likely to happen, but there was that feeling.

Fred came in and they ate. Marge was quiet.

'Nice tuna,' he said, holding up the bowl for her to take more.

'Same old stuff,' she said, but smiled. She looked over at him and noticed with a start that every hair on his head was grey. She stopped mid-bite and looked straight ahead. We're already old, she thought, why pretend? But to Fred she suddenly said, 'If the hibiscus come up as beautiful as your eyes, we'll throw a party!' Fred cocked his head to one side and smiled slightly.

They cleared up, then went through to the TV room to watch a soap or two.

When she woke up it was time to get the pictures. 'My goodness!' she said. Fred opened his eyes and mumbled something. Marge stood up quickly, pressed her hands cupped against her hair, and was on the front porch before she realised it was pouring rain. She stopped and put her hand out into it. Not too cold, she thought, good for the garden.

She put on her hat and coat and set out. The rain coursed off the edges of her hat in a weak waterfall, and by the time she got to the drugstore her trousers were soaked through.

As she approached, she caught a glimpse of herself again in the doors, darkened and out of focus from the sky and rain. She was a wreck, embarrassed, and once inside she wandered the aisles, hoping to dry off, and ended up eventually in the back of the store by foot preparations. The water ran off her into a puddle on the floor.

Arches, corns, calluses. Marge looked down at her own feet, ignoring the fresh wash of water from her hat which streamed onto the floor as a result. She wiggled her toes, cold and wet in her sneakers, considered herself lucky. She had feet like how she imagined children's must be – smooth, soft, the nails clear and unbroken. Her mother had believed that feet were the solid foundation of a solid life – or something like that, Marge thought. Marge and her sisters had spent their entire childhoods laced into 'sensible' shoes. Those shoes! Marge shivered now in the store to think of them – brown or black, laced snugly against her ankles. She was sure those shoes were to blame for having no dates in high school. Marge wondered what had ever happened to her friend Annette; sometimes she'd smuggled heeled pumps to Marge, but

Marge's feet always killed her, and she could never walk right in them, knees bent, bottom sticking out. Like a flamingo, she thought. She pursed her lips and sighed. Now it's worse; these days even without heels I look just like a duck.

She was relieved that Fred had never seemed to care as much as she did. He'd always seen the slimness of her ankles, even surrounded by supportive brown leather. He whistled the first time he saw her. She was delivering steaks and baked potatoes, waitressing in a local diner. 'Hey,' she heard, then a whistle.

She turned around, halfway back to the kitchen. 'What?' she said. She was annoyed, not cut out to be a waitress, too many things to do lined up in her head like seconds on a clock. 'What?' she said again, walking right over to him.

'Some ankles!'

That's it. That's all he said the first time they met.

In the store she looked down at her feet again, at the blue-white wet canvas of her shoes. She stretched her toes out flat inside them, then turned and went to the photography counter.

The same boy was there, on the phone, and after she'd been there a minute he cupped his hand over the mouthpiece and raised his eyebrows at her.

'Anderson?' she said.

He found the envelope and opened it up. 'I'm afraid there's a problem with some of the shots,' he said, 'maybe the film's a little old.' He showed one to Marge, and indeed, while most of the picture was under-exposed, there was some ring of red light, and a white blob in the middle. Maybe the table, Marge thought.

'Oh, that's all right,' she said, 'I'm sure it's my fault, really, and you know children, they don't hold still long enough . . .' The boy took her money, gave her change, and picked up the phone again. Marge opened, then closed her mouth, and walked out of the store.

The rain had slacked off to a drizzle so the way home was easier. She went through to the TV room and found Fred still sleeping in front of some ball game. She didn't understand the rules, but wherever it was, the weather was cold and the sun was shining.

She carried the photographs through to the kitchen, poured herself a glass of lemonade, and went into the smallest bedroom. One of the dining room chairs looked out the window and next to it was a round bedside table from years ago. This was her work room when she needed one, and like all the other rooms, it didn't have any curtains or decorations. Not for the first time, she wondered why it was they always had such high hopes. She took a sip of lemonade.

Marge unwrapped the photographs, flipped through them. The boy's right, she thought, every single one is flawed. Not even one of the baby. Finally she thought she found the two she was looking for – a figure in the centre of each, framed by darkness. She wished she'd taken more. It was just so difficult to tell.

She lined them up carefully on the windowsill. Beyond, out the window, it was dusk. She could see that the sun would finally shine soon, getting its short chance late in the day, the clouds moving eastward, over her head fast, like the disappearing hull of a ship.

She studied the pictures in the half-light. One of them looked like it had been swung overhead while developing, the chemicals run back and forth. The figure had an elongated face, very white, the mouth somehow drawn partly and grotesquely open, the hands and fingers drooping, practically touching what was once the ground. Can this be me? she thought.

The other had a yellowish tinge, but most of it was her fault entirely, she realised. She hadn't thought about the glare of the TV screen, and the flash had reflected, obscuring almost everything. The light seemed to extend one part of the figure, and when she leaned forward to see, she sat back quickly. The figure's forehead was blown up and out of proportion, as if pressed flat up against the inside of the TV.

But was I happy, she thought, am I smiling? She couldn't tell, and the little girl in the pictures could be doing anything, for all she knew; it could be any girl, even, she thought, not me at all.

She strained her eyes for a clue. She thought she could see bare legs, but the next minute she thought she remembered snow on the TV. Then she remembered a February day when it was seventy degrees and she went outside in shorts, played in the snow before it melted. Surely her father took a picture? Anything was possible. She looked for lace-up shoes, but the pictures didn't go down that far. She wished suddenly for her mother, dead twelve years now. Memory like a steel trap, Marge thought. She would be able to tell me everything.

When she opened her eyes again she couldn't move her head. She had fallen asleep, her chin sunk to her chest, her neck stiff. She raised her head with difficulty. The room was completely dark.

After a minute, she made out the window ahead of her, the early night sky. The photos were still on the sill, silhouetted; she could just see a point of light, the flash, shining from one of them.

Outside, the night was clear and bright, a half moon lighting up the yard, etching everything in blue and black and grey. The empty piles of stones waiting for palm trees looked like enormous pearls in this light, something precious, opalescent.

Everything looked underwater, in a still, clear world. Out of the corner of her eye she saw a figure come into the garden, dressed in white, opalescent as the stone-pearls. The figure moved slowly, deliberately, stooping to whisper, it seemed, to the plants, to Delilah. Maybe now she'll grow, Marge thought, and closed her eyes.

White skirts and sleeves floated around her. Wherever she passed, whatever she touched, blossomed life, waving up and out through weight of water, years in seconds. She smiled, turning, arms outstretched, setting the current in motion.

Whirlpool. Slippery grasses pulled her, pressed in. Open flowers swayed, wrapped around her. She spun down, heavy clothes twisting, branches holding her under. The night sky rippled, far away, then blackness.

Her eyes opened. The figure was gone, the night deepened, the garden as empty and flat as before.

Marge reached for the photos on the sill. She gathered them up and brought them into her lap. She felt their lightness, their lifelessness. She held her palms up empty, tilting them toward the moonlight. *You will have two children.* But the fortune teller had been looking in her eyes, at what she wanted, not at her hands, which were right after all.

Marge let her hands fall back into her lap, the pictures drifting to the floor.

'There you are,' Fred said, 'you okay?' He walked over and rested his hands on her shoulders. 'Pretty night.'

'Yes.' He'd startled her.

'Apparently Miami lost again,' he went on. 'I woke up and I'd missed the whole game.'

She put her hands on her thighs and stood up slowly. 'You hungry?'

'No,' he said, 'too tired. You?'

'No.'

'Let's turn in then.'

In bed she lay first with her head on his shoulder, his arm around her. He was smoking, and she wished he would stop some day soon because otherwise he was going to die and leave her alone in the big house.

'I know,' he said, 'I'll stop next year.'

'You and whose army,' she said automatically.

When he finished they turned onto their sides together, him curving around her. She couldn't sleep, and stared out the window, where in the distance she could just make out the orange glow from the lights of Fort Myers.

'Did you get those pictures?' he asked suddenly.

'Yes.' She paused. 'But you were right. It's not really me. I think I've just done my dumb thing again.'

'Well.' He sat up on one elbow, laid his cheek on her shoulder. 'It was worth a try.'

'I guess so.'

A couple of minutes passed.

'And the baby,' he said.

'Nothing.' She rolled onto her back, eyes shut tight. 'Whole film's messed up.'

After a minute he moved his hand from the bed and rested it lightly on her hip. She opened her eyes and looked up at him staring out the window, at his face set in all the old lines. In the dark his hair looked brown again, as brown as when they were first married, and his eyes, she could see his eyes reflecting the deep night sky, were the same colour blue.

Matthew Whyman

Spreading the Word

During the last breath of autumn, when the cold winds danced in the withering hemlock, and the angels were said to have been discovered by the riverbank, the entire village fell sick with an accursed affliction. The illness stiffened the residents' necks as rigid as tree trunks, arched their spines like bended twigs and forced their heads as far back as they would go.

The first whispers of the news to reach the neighbouring community told of a terrible tragedy in which diseased corpses lay prostrate in the gutters. Some said that the dead had been blinded by giant crows, who now circled above the rooftops in the hope that somebody might blunder into the village and fall prey to their razored beaks. Many had even heard that wolves were now roaming the streets, after the tang of blood had drifted in the breeze and penetrated the depths of the nearby forest.

The brave rescue party that did eventually storm the village, prepared for the worst with silver bullets and garlands of fresh garlic, were altogether relieved to realise, on seeing that the startled villagers were alive but not quite as well as they could have been, that the story had fallen victim to rumour.

Soon after their discovery, the sickly villagers were ordered by the neighbouring authorities to attend a meeting at the local hall one evening, where a suitable antidote might be formulated to remedy their problem.

The Chairman, sent to deal with the situation, now climbed onto the podium, gazed down at the forest of nervous faces and hushed for silence. Once the last murmurs had died away he told them that they were to explain, as accurately and clearly as they could, where the disease had originated and how it had arrived in their own fine homes. That way, the correct potion could be brewed and administered to rid them of their misery.

A few voices from the back rows piped up that the disease must have spawned from the angels, those dirty hussies with wings, for nobody had fallen ill for years on account of their pure and healthy lifestyle. A general air of agreement then embraced the gathering in the hall, despite their inability to nod.

The Chairman silenced them all once more and proposed that it might be prudent to start from the beginning, to decipher why they too had fallen foul of the disease. Before he could finish, however, a rumble of muttering welled up from the crowd. The Chairman quickly realised that he was going to have the devil of a job in deciphering any hard evidence from the vicious gossip and concocted hearsay that he might be given.

A group of anglers would have been the likeliest candidates to have stumbled upon the three heavenly outcasts. According to a number of unidentified sources, the angels were alleged to have been found crouched trembling in a gully by the riverbank, veiled by an early mist that had clung to the water's icy surface. The bravest fisherman would have stooped intrepidly towards the nearest angel, his eyes widening in surprise and awe on registering the porcelain sheen of her naked flesh.

He might have pressed her chilled hand into his palm and maybe wiped the white cloak of hoar frost from her shivering lips. If she had mouthed a warning to him, her lungs would have been so weakened, from what the villagers assumed had been a fall from grace, that her plea would have gone unnoticed.

Unfortunately nobody could confirm this point, although quite valid, so the Chairman promptly ignored it.

Instead, the villagers suggested that the fisherman might

have become entranced by the fading sparkle in her jaded eyes and shouted anxiously to his friends for help. If they had not already run away in fear, they might have come to his side and deliberated over what should be done with their unexpected catch.

Presumably then a group of fishermen, maybe six in number, would have tramped along the riverbank in a straggling line; each man supporting the head or the feet of their find and puffing hot breath into the still air. The three angels would have slumped weakly between their saviours, maybe trailing the tattered feathers of their broken wings in the sharp gravel of the path. If anybody had seen this sorry procession, they might well have been reminded of an army of hunters, returning to camp with their captive quarry.

The Chairman nodded in agreement, but resolved not to add this point to his notes after everybody fell silent when he asked if there had actually been any witnesses to the event.

The fishermen would have surely halted at the bridge that crosses the river, exhausted by the weight of their load but anxious to find help for the poorly angels. They could well have elected the nimblest fisherman to run to the police station in the village. Once there, he might have rushed in, colliding with the duty officer and bringing them both crashing to the floor.

Not surprisingly, if this had actually happened, the policeman would have listened to the garbled story that ensued and probably assumed that it was the drink talking. He might then have promptly ushered the joker down a parade of stone steps and invited him into a sparse but comfortable room, with a lovely view of the cobbled street outside and iron bars across the window.

The fisherman, perhaps slightly perplexed by such generous hospitality from somebody who was just a little angry, might have stepped, tripped or even been slung into the cell.

He could then have heard the chinking of heavy keys and a stiff reprimand from his jailor, perhaps reminding the poor man that his mother had the stench of the three-breasted Whore of Babylon. After that, the fisherman would probably have been left to sleep off the rogue effects of the drink that had never touched his lips.

Their recollection of the story was astoundingly clear, the Chairman remarked. Indeed, so much so that crystal would appear opaque by comparison. He was, however, a touch concerned that the harsh treatment dished out to the fisherman was hardly a fitting punishment for the crime of telling tales. Were they sure that a member of the local constabulary would have reacted in such a manner?

No doubt, the villagers pleaded, the copper's conduct had been shocking. Although they were only going on the word of the village grass, who also happened to have been banged up in the cells that night. For the price of a couple of jars, his information was not usually far off from the truth.

Unfortunately, the villagers were then forced to admit, the squealer who had divulged the news to them had since jumped bail and scarpered to the hills. Of course, now they thought back, the duty officer in question was indeed famous for his discerning nature.

The policeman then, despite being knocked to the floor by the arrival of the over-excited fisherman, would have been more likely to have simply brushed the dust from his tunic and listened carefully to the tale of the fallen angels. No doubt he might even have stifled a smirk when told of slight details, such as the huge wings that splayed from the shoulder-blades of the poor ladies.

At the end of his tale, the fisherman might well have stepped to the door, expecting the officer to follow him swiftly back to the river. The policeman, however, would have probably stretched his arms wide of his portly body and exclaimed that he was unlikely to believe a tale of such fabulous proportions, especially from the mouth of an angler. The officer might then have waved him from the station, having thanked him for providing such a glorious yarn to tell his own grandchildren.

The Chairman raised his hand for silence and demanded that the policeman, being sworn to tell the truth, should verify which story was correct.

The officer opted for the latter train of events. Despite never having even seen the fisherman that day, he was anxious not to confound the rest of their tale which might invite allegations of a cover-up.

The Chairman thanked him for his honesty and jotted some notes on a fresh sheet of paper.

The villagers then explained how it was quite likely that the fisherman would have tried to find help from someone dedicated to helping the sick and the needy. In which case, he would have dashed along the street to the doctor's surgery.

As he listened, the Chairman could not help but wonder that if the fisherman had been so delayed, his five friends who were waiting back at the riverbank might have questioned if he would ever return. Perhaps, even, the sight of the three angels had tortured their own wits to the extent that they had abandoned the sick creatures to the deep waters of the river. They might even have fled from the scene, having convinced each other that their catch was guarded from the shadows by a huge black hellhound with burning red eyes, flaming dribble and a craving for tasty anglers.

The Chairman silently pondered the options, but thought it more probable that the fishermen would have sat patiently awaiting the return of their messenger friend. It is unlikely that the sight of three fallen seraphs, lying helpless and naked, would provoke a man to turn away. No, they might even have been drawn closer, like thieves to a chest of treasure.

If the messenger had discovered the surgery open, he would

once again have made a breathless entrance and explained his story to the startled doctor. It was well-known, however, that the doctor was renowned for her pessimistic nature and even celebrated in the medical profession for her lack of patience. The villagers all agreed that she would have held her hand up to the mouth of the gibbering fisherman and swiftly re-primanded him for wasting her precious time.

What might the poor man have done if he had actually been in such a position? Surely his tale would be too fantastic to be believed by any other established members of the community. In which case, it was likely that he would have been thinking of returning to his friends at the bridge.

The Chairman straightened himself in his seat and slacken-ed his tie, anxious to hear what he believed would be the spiciest chapter of their tale.

Firstly though, the villagers suggested, the lone fisherman might have had a drink in a nearby tavern. Just a quick one, simply to calm his nerves and quench his thirst.

The Chairman clicked his tongue and urged the villagers to recount what had happened at the bridge.

Thinking that their friend might never return, the waiting fishermen would have brewed an alternative plan to deal with the angels. If they were of the entrepreneurial type, which the villagers had all secretly agreed to confirm, then the fishermen would have decided to sell the seraphs to the circus that had ar-rived some days before on the outskirts of the village. They would have been hard pressed to carry the birds there without a cart and horse, but the thought of the shameless riches that they might command for such a startling offer would have surely hastened their decision.

It would have been prudent, however, to wait until night-fall before setting off for the circus tent. If the fisherman had chosen to lug the three seraphs there in daylight, then they ran the risk of bumping into the Bishop's men, who would claim their catch as religious property and relieve them of their load.

Perhaps two fishermen would have elected to inform the ringmaster before presenting their goods. Maybe a feather had then been plucked from the celestial catch, as evidence of their existence, before the two salesmen set off from the bridge.

The ringmaster would probably have been found in the caravan belonging to the rubber woman. The chances were that she would have been entertaining him with her elastic contortions and life-threatening strangleholds; a performance that she was purported to put on as a special display to fulfil his indulgent desires. The fishermen would probably have headed straight for the caravan and knocked politely at the door.

The ringmaster, if he was inside at the time, would have leapt up from the bed. This might have been tricky, however, for he would probably have had to untangle himself from her supple legs while carefully avoiding the stinging nettles that he liked to have strewn over the sheets. If the rubber woman's show had almost reached its searing climax, he would also have had to yank his hands free from the shackles bolted to the roof.

This, the villagers supposed, could have taken a while.

Eventually, after presumably throwing on his bright red waistcoat and top hat, the ringmaster would have opened the door to the fisherman, blushed the shade of his meagre garments and covered the great lion tamer between his legs with a tea towel. He might also have been entirely speechless, thinking that the secret of his sordid vice was out and would soon be common knowledge. The secret, however, had already been exposed after the observant villagers had remarked upon his over-zealous use of the whip when the circus had last come to town.

Confronted by the two fishermen, however, the ringmaster would have had no choice but to whip up an excuse, demanding to know why he had been interrupted from working on new material for the show. The fishermen, aware of the value of their prize, would have explained the situation, proudly presenting him with the long feather and awaiting an offer. The ringmaster, wise to the existence of such creatures from his exotic travels with the circus, would perhaps have invited them inside to discuss business.

By this time, the rubber woman could have wrapped a moleskin shawl around her lithe body and might perhaps have been making a pot of tea for the three businessmen. The ringmaster could have offered, say, ten pounds for the three angels, to which the fishermen would have spat upon the floor and scoffed indignantly at such a paltry offer. If the reputation of the ringmaster was unknown to the fishermen, which was likely, then they would not have been aware that he already owned a cage of twenty angels. The ringmaster had purchased the birds in a distant land, in exchange for what the villagers claimed was an old nag with a spike glued to its head that he had passed off as a priceless unicorn.

Why should he want three stinking hags that had been found in a river? He possessed the most beautiful specimens the world had ever seen, seraphs who could satisfy any man, for the highest price.

The two fishermen could have realised that the deal was off. They might have swigged down their tea and presumably refused to have their fortunes read from the dregs. They would almost certainly have turned down the ringmaster's very enticing offer of half an hour with his feathered nymphs, in exchange for their silence regarding his embarrassing carnal secrets. Instead, the fishermen would have probably bid them both goodbye, apologised for the interruption and left the caravan clutching nothing but one sorry feather.

No! There must be a fault in this story somewhere, the Chairman declared. It would be unlikely that two men with the potential for making easy money would have abandoned their quest. No, if the ringmaster had mentioned that he could sell his own sweet angels to men with the highest bid, then a similar idea would surely have occurred to one of the fishermen.

The villagers asked for a moment to try and remember, whispering words that the Chairman was unable to make out.

Sure there was more! they then chirped. Once the six men were all together again, they were bound to have thought of selling their catch to the local sin house. That would be very likely, as Madame had been on the lookout for new blood since most of her girls had blossomed and run away to the higher wages of the cities.

The Chairman then asked the villagers to verify that it had been *six* fishermen that ventured to the brothel.

Of course, claimed the villagers, had they ever misled him before?

If that was the case, the Chairman pointed out, then surely somebody was missing?

If the first messenger had succumbed to the lure of the ale, the villagers conveniently remembered, then he would have surely recounted the events of the day to the old soaks who frequented the village tavern. The tale might have been worthy of a good hour's drinking, before somebody else could provide a new story to slake their thirsty imagination. The fisherman might have decided to stay and listen to the personally authenticated claims concerning tidal waves, shipwrecks, and feats of levitation. Or, as is more likely, he would have remembered his five friends and staggered back to the bridge.

The Chairman banged his fist on the table and demanded to know which it was to be.

The villagers thought for a moment and opted for the latter. That way, they hoped the Chairman might believe their tale when they told him that all six anglers would have been reunited at the bridge by nightfall.

The fisherman accused of drinking the day away was about to plead that if he had actually been at the tavern, he must have been too sozzled to remember anything about it. He said nothing though, having noticed that the Chairman was engrossed in a startling burst of note-taking.

While scribbling down his comments and suspicions, the Chairman had begun to entertain the possibility that a cart and horse might have been fetched from the fisherman who lived nearest to the river. This would have been most likely, assuming that the plan to sell the angels to Madame had been agreed upon after hearing of the ringmaster's price for his own flock. When he mentioned this possibility, the villagers quickly flattered the Chairman for his remarkable insight, for they were just about to say the same thing in any case.

Madame would have been at her bedroom window around nightfall, presumably there to wedge her ample folds into a tantalisingly petite bodice. Having completed that ritual struggle, she would probably have drawn the red curtains and lit the candle to signal her opening hours.

If Madame really had been upstairs, then she would have seen the fishermen arriving outside with the cart. If this was so, she would have covered up her wares as a matter of decency, swiftly donned a spot of rouge and shuffled downstairs in her velvet slippers to meet them.

The fishermen could have doffed their caps out of respect and invited themselves inside to discuss the business at hand.

The Chairman raised his pen from the paper for a moment. Surely, he proposed, the fishermen would have enticed Madame outside to exhibit their load on the cart. Perhaps they would have drawn back the tarpaulin wrap with a majestic sweep, exposing their magnificent catch and instantly seducing Madame into parting with her cash.

The Chairman was not surprised to hear from the villagers

that his guess had been correct, except for one slight problem.

Madame might have been indignant when confronted by the three dead angels, sprawled in a manner unsuited to their blessed status.

What is this then? she would have scoffed, possibly lifting a limp wing between her impeccably varnished fingernails.

The fishermen might have looked at each other in horror, realising that the frozen ruts along the journey had proved too much for the weak creatures.

Madame could then have remarked that she would not have taken the angels had they been alive, for it was plain that they had been near to handing in their haloes when first discovered. In any case, only a few of her esteemed clientele would have been interested in such shabby birds. Maybe she knew of a few shady devils that would be excited by a dead one, but no. She was, after all, a respectable lady.

Instead, Madame would probably have advised the fishermen to take the deceased away and give them the final honour of a decent burial. She could then have paused to think about the consequences of her own involvement, should tongues become twitchy. If so, Madame would have instructed the fishermen to get rid of the buggers quick sharp, with nothing short of a good burning.

As the fishermen searched their pockets for matches, Madame, whose business mind far outstripped her six potential customers, could have silently planned a means of profiting from the situation. She might then have suggested that her own domestic, a young ragamuffin who acted as chauffeur, chef and dresser to her girls, should drive the celestial stiffs out to the forest in her own fur-lined carriage. Once there, he could carry out a spot of cremation and it would only cost the gentlemen a mere ten pounds for her trouble.

The fishermen, who would probably have been eager to get rid of the three corpses, might well have agreed to Madame's generous suggestion. Had this happened, she would have gracefully placed thumb and forefinger between her lips and sent forth a piercing whistle.

On hearing the shrill blast, the young waif would have scampered up from the cellar and presented himself at her disposal. With the help of the six fishermen, the boy might then have heaved the perished angels from cart to carriage, leapt onto the front seat, grabbed the reins and disappeared in a spiral of dust and a crack of the lash.

The fishermen would have stood and silently pondered the loss of their catch, assuming that Madame's four fearless stallions actually had thundered her carriage across the moonlit fields.

Regrettably, nobody in the hall could testify to having seen the flames during the night in question. The villagers did assume, however, that the scarlet glow of the fire would have been sufficient to guide the angels on their return journey.

After such a long day, the fishermen would surely have been ready for playtime, especially if presented to Madame's six remaining girls. They might have finished preening themselves by this time and slunk downstairs to make their introductions.

Yes, this all seems quite probable, the Chairman reflected. Just to be sure, he then inquired whether those who pointed the accusing fingers were certain of their facts. After all, this was a matter that held the reputations of six men, Madame, her fine young girls and a growing lad in the balance.

The villagers were horrified at this suggestion. They immediately retorted that any allegations were based upon the evidence discovered that night, by the wife of one of the fishermen. Believing that her husband's cart had been stolen from the courtyard, she had searched the dark streets and discovered the empty wagon, tethered to the gates of the brothel. On hearing a familiar shriek of laughter come from inside the seedy den, she had stolen a peek through a chink in the curtains.

Within minutes, the scandalous word had reached the other wives.

When the six men had eventually returned to their respective homes that night, tired and poorer but with a glow in their cheeks, every one of them was confronted by a rusty slicing tool found propped against their doorsteps. After reading the threatening notes pinned to the blades, the wayward fishermen had each felt compelled to sleep in their sculleries, with one eye firmly open and both legs firmly crossed.

Finding their tackle to be intact the following morning, the fishermen were fortunate to have each given the same excuse to their wives, which they were now obliged to recount to the Chairman.

Their tale told of how they had merely dropped in at Madame's establishment on their way home from the day's fishing, just for a quick cup of tea and a natter with her fine ladies. While relaxing in front of the fire, discussing the latest revelations in the fields of philosophy and astronomy, Madame had very kindly offered to scrub the smell of the riverwater from their clothes.

The fisherman who owned the cart then pleaded to the Chairman that he had only taken it to carry the fish from the river and up to the market. He even produced the receipt for the fifteen pounds that he had made from the day's sale.

The fisherman's wife still had her suspicions however, as did the Chairman. He pointed out that a crucial point had been overlooked, or withheld, regarding an episode that might have occurred back at the bridge.

At some point during that day, the Chairman began, after their colleagues had left the riverbank to find help or make money, the salacious thoughts of the three remaining fishermen must surely have got the better of their sensibilities.

Perhaps they had each turned to one another and hinted at the mischief they might indulge in. Eventually, one of them might have been brave enough to propose that they drag the seraphs under the bridge to partake in some dirty games.

If the filthy seed of their lust really had begun to flourish, then each fisherman would have chosen the angel that could fulfil them most. In this case, it would not have been long before their crumpled petals of desire had been gathered into trembling arms and heaved off into the shadows.

This would seem to have been most likely, the Chairman proclaimed, everything now fits into place.

The villagers quickly agreed with the Chairman and scorned the fishermen with vulgar curses. When he remarked that the story did not explain why they all bore the symptoms of the same affliction, the Chairman received no answer.

Despite persistently claiming never to have clapped eyes on any angels, the six fishermen could no longer muster the spirit to protest their innocence. Sure, they had been fishing by the river all day, as they did every day. True, they finally admitted, Madame had also entertained them exceptionally well that evening. She had even refused their cash, requiring only the finest catch from their fish hooks in payment for the pleasure of her services.

Perhaps the ringmaster might have been able to clear their names, especially as he had never even seen the fishermen before, nor, for that matter had he ever heard of a rubber woman.

Unfortunately for the accused, however, the circus had since upped sticks and departed, for business had been bad after the disease had hit the village. The ailing audience that did show up had just complained that because of their cricked and stricken condition, they were only able to see the trapeze artists and just a glimpse of the human cannonball as she was propelled through the roof of the big top.

Madame herself would have sworn on her good name that she too had never seen the angels. Unfortunately for the fishermen though, she had since grabbed the boy and her girls and travelled to the docks in search of the bastard whom she suspected of first giving them the dose in question.

Even if she had been present that night to testify the innocence of her customers, she would have made little impact. The rest of the village were so convinced by their own rumours that nobody questioned whether the angels had actually existed. Indeed, if their tale really was all fibs, then not one of them could remember who had conjured up the story in the first place.

The fishermen blushed deeply, convinced that somehow they had been the original sprinklers of the disease. The villagers, however, took no notice of the shame that they betrayed. They too were all struck by varying degrees of the same guilt. Like the fishermen, their own moral fibre had also frayed over the previous weeks, as it had done since they could all remember.

Indeed, the rumours that had created the story only came into existence when each villager began to fall prey to the clutches of the illness that Madame and the six fishermen had already contracted.

As each person began to feel a tension in the neck, various tales had been cobbled together that staved off any suspicion regarding their own clandestine away-games; facts that would be of particular interest to their respective spouses.

The villagers avoided the suspicious eyes of the Chairman. Instead, wives stared at neighbours' husbands, husbands stared at friends' wives who in turn glanced back at neighbours. The policeman stared at the doctor who knew one of the fishermen better than she should have done. Best friends stared at one other as did the fishermen, who would have stared at Madame, had she been present. The villagers would not have been able to stare at each other at all, if it was not for the mirror that had been fixed to the rafters of the hall to assist the progress of the meeting.

Although their tale was questionable, it had never occurred to the villagers that the disease might have reached each one of them in a more innocent fashion.

Not one person suggested that the affliction could have been transmitted by air, or maybe spawned in the water.

Nobody considered that the disease might even have been spread by mouth.

Maybe the villagers had exposed themselves to infection when they left their doorsteps to gossip about the fishermen and Madame's fine girls.

Perhaps, if they had remained in their houses, everyone might have avoided the evil touch of the germs.

The villagers, however, had already recounted their own convenient conclusions to the Chairman.

The meeting finished well after nightfall with a vague promise by the Chairman of the arrival of the antidote in the coming days. Despite their belief that they would soon be cured, the villagers remained inside the hall. Secret lovers glanced nervously at one other and prayed that they would each remain silent.

None of the villagers were willing to leave, for they all knew that in their poorly condition, they would have no choice but to stare straight up at the heavens.

The Chairman donned his cap and stepped out into the deserted village square. He plodded homeward along the river path, troubled by the possibility that the story given during the meeting might not have been entirely truthful.

Lost in thought as he sauntered along, he failed to realise that he had taken a wrong turning at the bridge. It was some time before the anguished howls of a wolf in the forest awoke him from his ponderings. The Chairman then realised that he was now further from home than when he had first set off.

Rather than head straight back, he decided to rest for a

while, puff on a smoke and weigh up the evidence. That way, he could present his conclusions to the authorities at first light.

Perching himself on a tree stump, he noticed how the stars in the sky reflected so clearly on the iced waters of the river, they could almost be trapped beneath its frozen surface. As he gazed on, he sensed a febrile hush all around, as if the very reeds that hugged the riverbank were too sick to sing in the breeze. Although the morning sun was beginning to peek over the distant tree-tops of the forest, the birds too remained silent in their nests.

When the darkness began to recede into dawn, the fresh light of the day soon roused the Chairman from his thoughts. He stood up, resolved that it was their own problem if the antidote failed to work and yawned loudly.

As he stretched himself, he suddenly spotted a single feather that had been trampled into the gravel path.

The Chairman peered a little closer, but was drawn to a sight away from the feather that seized the breath from his lungs in an instant. For there lay the cause of the eerie silence. There, crouched trembling in the gully by the riverbank, veiled by an early mist that clung to the water's icy surface.

Bravely, the Chairman lowered his arm to the only one of the three creatures who still appeared to be breathing. He pressed her chilled hand into his palm before wiping the white cloak of hoar frost from her shivering lips. She tried to mouth a warning to him, but her face and neck were too stiff to move. The Chairman stooped lower to offer his ear a little closer and when he finally reached home, he swore to his incredulous superiors that with her dying breath, an angel had told him not to eat the fish.

biographies

Sarah Gracie was born in 1961 in Bahrain, and grew up in Scotland. After taking a First in English Literature at University College, Oxford, she taught in prisons and psychiatric hospitals. She has won prizes in the Arvon Poetry and Ian St James short story competitions.

Adam Belgrave Campbell was born in 1963 to parents with mixed Jamaican and British ancestry. He grew up in Jamaica and Zambia and went through secondary and further education in London. He read Civil Engineering at Imperial College and worked in the oil industry for six years. He is currently working on a novel.

August Braxton was born in 1959 in Newcastle-Upon-Tyne and lives in South London. *Full Things Spill* is his first novel. He is currently working on a second.

Jane Harris has lived most of her life in Glasgow. She started writing in Portugal, where she was working as a teacher. Her work is published in various anthologies and magazines, including *Chapman*, *New Writing Scotland* 8 and 9, *Brando's Hat*, *West Coast Magazine* and *The Crazy Jig*, published by Polygon. She is currently completing a short story collection and working on a novel and a screenplay.

Karin Hurst was educated at Nottingham and Oxford Universities and Central School of Speech and Drama, London. She lectures in English literature and theatre. She is currently writing a novel, *Touching Stones*, some short stories and a radio series.

David Rhymes was born in Nottingham in 1965, and studied English and American literature at the university of Warwick. Since graduation, he has worked as an EFL teacher in Spain and as a musician. He began writing in late 1990 and is currently working on a novel.

Kirkham Jackson was born in Great Harwood, Lancashire in 1960. He studied theatre at Dartington College of Arts in Devon and spent seven years in London, writing and performing in a number of bands. Since 1990 he has been concentrating on writing short stories.

Simon Christmas read Philosophy at Caius College, Cambridge . He wrote his first novel while at university, and contributed chapters to an introduction to twentieth century European philosophy. He is currently working on a new novel and a television script.

Joanne Gooding was born in Malta and educated in the UK. She is now resident in London, where she has worked as a freelance film animator since graduating from Art School. Her first novel, *Video Games*, was published by Piatkus Books in 1989. She is currently working on a small screen adaptation of her second novel. The first draft of a third novel is near completion.

Katherine Eban Finklestein grew up in Brooklyn, New York. She graduated from Brown University in 1988 with a BA in English literature, then attended Oxford University on a Rhodes scholarship. She graduated in 1991 with an M. Phil in seventeenth century English literature and is now living in Norwich. She is currently writing a screenplay, a series of essays about England, and completing *Mortal Taste*, her first novel.

Neil Church was born in Brighton in 1963. He read English at St Catherine's College, Oxford, graduating in 1986, and has since pursued interests in comedy writing and music. His satirical novel, *The New Puritans*, is to be published by Aidan Ellis in February 1993.

Tasha Pym was born in 1969 and received her first degree in Creative Arts from Nottingham Polytechnic. She has had work produced for stage and radio and is currently writing her first novel.

Archie Clifford was born in Wolverhampton in 1955. He worked in local government, civil engineering, industrial welding, and a number of other jobs, before returning to full time education in 1983 (BA Hons in Illustration at Brighton Polytechnic 1984-7) He is currently working on a novel, *Quartet in a Flat*, from which his extract is taken.

C M Rafferty is Irish and studied at Lester Pearson College, Canada and Trinity College, Dublin. She is currently working on a collection of short stories and a novel.

Patricia Debney was born in Texas and grew up in Southwestern Virginia. She graduated from Oberlin College in Ohio in 1986, and has been living in England since 1988. She is currently working on a collection of short stories and completing a novel.

Matthew Whyman was born in 1969 and brought up in Berkhamsted, Hertfordshire. He was educated at Bournemouth Polytechnic and now lives in France, where he is an English teacher. He is currently writing his first novel, *Honey Mouth*, based upon the travels of the eighteenth century explorer, Mungo Park. A short story, *Revelations*, will be published in *New Writing 2* (Minerva, January 1993).